MY NAME IS ARAM

By WILLIAM SAROYAN

ONE secret of this completely charming book is in its very first and very last sentences. I won't spoil your pleasure by pulling them out and quoting them here; I'm simply telling you to read them carefully, and in their proper places, first and last, and see how they compose and frame and summarize the book's quality.

It gives me a peculiar and special pleasure that our committee chose this book. It is the kind of thing that might so easily *not* have been chosen. Suppose we w e r e looking only f o r some obvious kind of skill or success: let's say a thundering big costume novel, dense with historical visas and velvet pantaloons; or an important biography; or a crystal carboy of political assurance; or whatever. Any such book would be simple to recognize and acclaim. And here is a little series of childhood memories, describing the imaginative life of an Armenian boy in California (a kind of immigrant Penrod) done with quiet strokes of humor and grace. Would you not have thought that perhaps a hardworking committee might h a v e said Yes, delightful but maybe not important? Yet that same committee were unanimous in thinking this one of the most satisfying and meaningful books that have come before us in some time. Many a heavy tome of history and economics holds less of what America deeply means.

It is a special pleasure, too, because about six years ago your reviewer was assigned to comment in this place on Mr. Saroyan's first book. He did so with enthusiasm but also pointed out some particular dangers and temptations a writer of Mr. Saroyan's unusual talent would have to face. He has faced them and for the most part outwitted them. He tells us in his pleasant preface that these stories, drawn out of his own boyhood memories around Fresno, California, were written "without effort, strain, or any of the other kinds of wretchedness said to be experienced by writers." In every way these innocent and guileful stories show that happy feeling of frank lightness and ease. Like Cousin Mourad (in the opening story of the Beautiful White Horse) who had a way with horses, or farmers, or dogs, or what not, Mr. Saroyan has a way with memories. He has the exquisite high-fidelity-selection of the unconscious dramatist who knows by instinct what to remember. And if you want to meditate on social significances, ask yourself what America would be like if our natural Angloid heaviness of temper had not been fermented and souffléd by s u c h diverse racial strains? The picture of the Armenian families living in the fruit and vineyard regions of California is just one tiny odd-shaped piece in the great foreign-genius jigsaw pattern that fertilizes American art. Mr. Saroyan has the Asia-minor gift for telling a tale perfectly.

So you will read with delight, and with some humility too, of "the proud and angry Saroyans" (or Garoghlanians if you prefer) and their struggles with American civilization. How excellent is sad Uncle Jorgi who was happy when there wasn't any job in the melon fields and he and the boy could sit for a month in an empty house cooking rice and playing the zither. You will read aloud, perhaps, the dialogue of the grandfather and grandmother; t h e magnificent grandfather who disbelieved what he found in books and when the old lady talked too much would threaten "the back of my hand is on its way to your mouth." Or Uncle Melik who insisted on planting pomegranate trees where they could not possibly grow, on a sandy desert "away over to hell and gone at the foot of the Sierra Nevada." It was impossible for the orchards, Uncle Melik imagined, but it was "a region of loneliness, emptiness, truth and dignity. It was nature at its proudest, dryest, loneliest and loveliest." And if you will stop to think a moment—I often wonder how many readers ever do?—you will see that Saroyan himself, in some of his most moving plays, has been trying the same thing. He took the arid soil of Broadway theatres and actually made pomegranates grow there.

Anyone who has ever been a child will relish the story of the Fifty Yard Dash. The twelve year old boy Aram—who is not much different from Mr. Saroyan himself — clipped a coupon of Lionel Strongfort's advertisement offering to make him strong and invincible. He finally wangled three dollars f r o m a mystical and unwilling uncle to pay for Mr. Strongfort's secret. Armed with this, and in spite of some lively criticism from the grandmother, he thought to win the Longfellow School's track meet. He ran, in his own mind, faster than any human being ever ran before. . . . But read the story as Mr. Saroyan himself tells it. It is more important even than the g r e a t Secret offered by Lionel Strongfort, the man in the leopard skin. It is the secret of every imaginative child. It is the history of every artist.

So gradually, and with ruminating delight, you will come to the last episode, where the melancholy man in overalls in Salt Lake City tells young Aram Garoghlanian another great secret. That is the secret that makes this book beautiful in its own modest and insinuating way. Here Mr. Saroyan justifies all the promise we predicted for him and shows himself the grown and many-colored artist; the genuine poet in prose, and spokesman for the youth of the world.

CHRISTOPHER MORLEY

In accordance with a suggestion made by a number of our subscribers, this monthly reprint from the Book-of-the-Month Club *News* is printed in this format so that it can be pasted, if desired, to the flyleaf of the book.

PRINTED IN U. S. A.

My Name Is Aram

MY NAME IS ARAM

by

WILLIAM SAROYAN

ILLUSTRATED
BY
Don Freeman

WILLIAM SAROYAN

My Name
Is Aram

ILLUSTRATED BY DON FREEMAN

HARCOURT, BRACE AND COMPANY, NEW YORK

Typography by Robert Josephy
PRINTED IN THE UNITED STATES OF AMERICA
BY H. WOLFF BOOK MFG. CO., INC., NEW YORK

Acknowledgment is made to the following periodicals in which some of these stories first appeared: *Esquire, The Atlantic Monthly, The London Evening Standard, Hairenik, Harper's, Collier's, Story, The Coast,* and *The New Yorker.*

NOTE

The writer returns these pleasant memories to the world at Fresno, California, from the year 1915 to the year 1925 (from the time he was seven years old and was beginning to inhabit the world as a specific person to the time he was seventeen years old and had forsaken his native valley for some of the rest of the world), and to the members of his immediate family in that world during those years. That is to say, to the ugly little city containing the large comic world, and to the proud and angry Saroyans containing all humanity. While no character in this book is a portrait of any real person living or dead, as the saying is, neither is any person in this book a creation of fiction. No member of my family will be able to find himself in any one person in this book, but at the same time none will be able to find himself wholly *absent* from any one of them. If this is true of us, it is also probably true of everybody else, which in the opinion of the writer is proper.

As for the world at Fresno, California, if some

of it is gone, so is some of the writer's youthful impatience with it. It was, as a matter of fact, and probably still is, as good a town as any in the world for a writer to be born into, being neither too large nor too small, too urban or too rural, too progressive or too backward, too athletic or too lame, too intelligent or too stupid, too arid or too lush, but in all these things, as well as in all others, and in several unknown anywhere else in the world, so delicately, so nicely, and so delightfully balanced as to give the spirit of the growing writer almost exactly the right proportions of severity and warmth, and firmness and flexibility; the mind a critical and yet compassionate understanding; and the impulse to write an abundance of material by nature so rich in the elements of comedy as to require little or no labor to select and chronicle. Consequently, the writing of this book, more than the writing of any of the writer's other books, has been without effort, strain, or any of the other kinds of wretchedness said to be experienced by writers as eager, if not more eager than this writer to send a message down the ages, as the saying is. On the contrary, the writer simply wrote the words while his spirit enjoyed their meaning.

Note

If the truth is told, the writer, even as he wrote, was less writer than reader, and had as little idea as to what was coming next, for sure, as you are likely to have. The writer does not belong to any school of writing and does not believe this manner of writing is the way to get a message to go high-rolling down the ages, but at the same time, for a less ambitious intention, he can find no fault with the method, other than, perhaps, that it tends to make the writer unqualified for membership in The Authors' League of America (Inc.).

The writer wishes to express his gratitude to the two American editors who urged him to buckle down and write this book: Mr. Edward Weeks, editor of *The Atlantic Monthly,* and Mr. Edward J. O'Brien, editor of *The Best Short Stories* and *The Yearbook of the American Short Story.* Mr. Weeks accomplished his urging in the manner most pleasing to the writer: by accepting one of the stories for *The Atlantic Monthly,* and soon afterward by accepting the next one written, and not long after that, by accepting several more, until, in all, six or seven of the stories appeared in *The Atlantic Monthly.* Mr. O'Brien simply said, Write more about the Armenians. To which,

Note

if memory does not fail him, the writer made the following reply: Yes, sir.

As far as I am able to tell, what this book is is the story of an American boy named Aram Garoghlanian. I do not pretend that the story has any plot, and I hereby give fair warning that nothing extraordinary is going to happen in it.

The way to pronounce that name is to say *Gar,* pause, *oghlan,* slight pause, *ian.* The name is an Armenian name made of two Turkish words, *gar,* meaning dark or possibly black, and *oghlan,* meaning, unmistakably and without qualification, son; *ian,* meaning, naturally, of that tribe. In short, Garoghlanian Aram, meaning Aram of the dark or black sons. Which may not be a matter of the very greatest importance to anybody this year, but may take on an appropriately modest importance later on. As to whether or not the writer himself is Aram Garoghlanian, the writer cannot very well say. He will, however, say that he is not, certainly, *not* Aram Garoghlanian.

WILLIAM SAROYAN

San Francisco.
June 30, 1940.

CONTENTS

THE SUMMER OF THE

BEAUTIFUL WHITE HORSE

ONE day back there in the good old days when I was nine and the world was full of every imaginable kind of magnificence, and life was still a delightful and mysterious dream, my cousin Mourad, who was considered crazy by everybody who knew him except me, came to my house at four in the morning and woke me up by tapping on the window of my room.

Aram, he said.

I jumped out of bed and looked out the window.

I couldn't believe what I saw.

It wasn't morning yet, but it was summer and with daybreak not many minutes around the corner of the world it was light enough for me to know I wasn't dreaming.

My cousin Mourad was sitting on a beautiful white horse.

I stuck my head out of the window and rubbed my eyes.

Yes, he said in Armenian. It's a horse. You're not dreaming. Make it quick if you want to ride.

I knew my cousin Mourad enjoyed being alive more than anybody else who had ever fallen into the world by mistake, but this was more than even I could believe.

In the first place, my earliest memories had been memories of horses and my first longings had been longings to ride.

This was the wonderful part.

In the second place, we were poor.

This was the part that wouldn't permit me to believe what I saw.

We were poor. We had no money. Our whole tribe was poverty-stricken. Every branch of the Garoghlanian family was living in the most amazing and comical poverty in the world. Nobody could understand where we ever got money enough to keep us with food in our bellies, not even the old men of the family. Most important of all, though, we were famous for our honesty. We had been famous for our honesty for something like eleven centuries, even when we had been the wealthiest family in what we liked to think was the world. We were proud first, honest next, and after that we believed in right and wrong. None of us would take advantage of anybody in the world, let alone steal.

Consequently, even though I could *see* the horse, so magnificent; even though I could *smell* it, so lovely; even though I could *hear* it breathing, so exciting; I couldn't *believe* the horse had anything to do with my cousin Mourad or with me or with any of the other members of our family, asleep or awake, because I *knew* my cousin Mourad couldn't have *bought* the horse, and if he couldn't have bought it he must have *stolen* it, and I refused to believe he had stolen it.

No member of the Garoghlanian family could be a thief.

I stared first at my cousin and then at the horse. There was a pious stillness and humor in each of them which on the one hand delighted me and on the other frightened me.

Mourad, I said, where did you steal this horse?

Leap out of the window, he said, if you want to ride.

It was true, then. He *had* stolen the horse. There was no question about it. He had come to invite me to ride or not, as I chose.

Well, it seemed to me stealing a horse for a ride was not the same thing as stealing something else, such as money. For all I knew, maybe it wasn't stealing at all. If you were crazy about horses the way my cousin Mourad and I were, it wasn't stealing. It wouldn't become stealing until we offered to sell the horse, which of course I knew we would never do.

Let me put on some clothes, I said.

All right, he said, but hurry.

I leaped into my clothes.

I jumped down to the yard from the window and leaped up onto the horse behind my cousin Mourad.

That year we lived at the edge of town, on Walnut Avenue. Behind our house was the country: vineyards, orchards, irrigation ditches, and country roads. In less than three minutes we were on Olive Avenue, and then the horse began to trot. The air was new and lovely to breathe. The feel of the horse running was wonderful. My cousin Mourad who was considered one of the craziest members of our family began to sing. I mean, he began to roar.

Every family has a crazy streak in it somewhere, and my cousin Mourad was considered the nat-

6

ural descendant of the crazy streak in our tribe. Before him was our uncle Khosrove, an enormous man with a powerful head of black hair and the largest mustache in the San Joaquin Valley, a man so furious in temper, so irritable, so impatient that he stopped anyone from talking by roaring, *It is no harm; pay no attention to it.*

That was all, no matter what anybody happened to be talking about. Once it was his own son Arak running eight blocks to the barber shop where his father was having his mustache trimmed to tell him their house was on fire. This man Khosrove sat up in the chair and roared, It is no harm; pay no attention to it. The barber said, But the boy says your house is on fire. So Khosrove roared, Enough, it is no harm, I say.

My cousin Mourad was considered the natural descendant of this man, although Mourad's father was Zorab, who was practical and nothing else. That's how it was in our tribe. A man could be the father of his son's flesh, but that did not mean that he was also the father of his spirit. The distribution of the various kinds of spirit of our tribe had been from the beginning capricious and vagrant.

We rode and my cousin Mourad sang. For all

anybody knew we were still in the old country where, at least according to some of our neighbors, we belonged. We let the horse run as long as it felt like running.

At last my cousin Mourad said, Get down. I want to ride alone.

Will you let me ride alone? I said.

That is up to the horse, my cousin said. Get down.

The *horse* will let me ride, I said.

We shall see, he said. Don't forget that I have a way with a horse.

Well, I said, any way you have with a horse, I have also.

For the sake of your safety, he said, let us hope so. Get down.

All right, I said, but remember you've got to let me try to ride alone.

I got down and my cousin Mourad kicked his heels into the horse and shouted, *Vazire,* run. The horse stood on its hind legs, snorted, and burst into a fury of speed that was the loveliest thing I had ever seen. My cousin Mourad raced the horse across a field of dry grass to an irrigation ditch, crossed the ditch on the horse, and five minutes later returned, dripping wet.

8

The Beautiful White Horse

The sun was coming up.

Now it's my turn to ride, I said.

My cousin Mourad got off the horse.

Ride, he said.

I leaped to the back of the horse and for a moment knew the awfulest fear imaginable. The horse did not move.

Kick into his muscles, my cousin Mourad said. What are you waiting for? We've got to take him back before everybody in the world is up and about.

I kicked into the muscles of the horse. Once again it reared and snorted. Then it began to run. I didn't know what to do. Instead of running across the field to the irrigation ditch the horse ran down the road to the vineyard of Dikran Halabian where it began to leap over vines. The horse leaped over seven vines before I fell. Then it continued running.

My cousin Mourad came running down the road.

I'm not worried about you, he shouted. We've got to get that horse. You go this way and I'll go this way. If you come upon him, be kindly. I'll be near.

I continued down the road and my cousin

Mourad went across the field toward the irrigation ditch.

It took him half an hour to find the horse and bring him back.

All right, he said, jump on. The whole world is awake now.

What will we do? I said.

Well, he said, we'll either take him back or hide him until tomorrow morning.

He didn't sound worried and I knew he'd hide him and not take him back. Not for a while, at any rate.

Where will we hide him? I said.

I know a place, he said.

How long ago did you steal this horse? I said.

It suddenly dawned on me that he had been taking these early morning rides for some time and had come for me this morning only because he knew how much I longed to ride.

Who said anything about stealing a horse? he said.

Anyhow, I said, how long ago did you begin riding every morning?

Not until this morning, he said.

Are you telling the truth? I said.

Of course not, he said, but if we are found out,

that's what you're to say. I don't want both of us
to be liars. All you know is that we started riding
this morning.

All right, I said.

He walked the horse quietly to the barn of a
deserted vineyard which at one time had been the
pride of a farmer named Fetvajian. There were
some oats and dry alfalfa in the barn.

We began walking home.

It wasn't easy, he said, to get the horse to behave so nicely. At first it wanted to run wild, but,
as I've told you, I have a way with a horse. I can
get it to want to do anything *I* want it to do.
Horses understand me.

How do you do it? I said.

I have an understanding with a horse, he said.

Yes, but what sort of an understanding? I said.

A simple and honest one, he said.

Well, I said, I wish I knew how to reach an
understanding like that with a horse.

You're still a small boy, he said. When you get
to be thirteen you'll know how to do it.

I went home and ate a hearty breakfast.

That afternoon my uncle Khosrove came to
our house for coffee and cigarettes. He sat in the
parlor, sipping and smoking and remembering

the old country. Then another visitor arrived, a farmer named John Byro, an Assyrian who, out of loneliness, had learned to speak Armenian. My mother brought the lonely visitor coffee and tobacco and he rolled a cigarette and sipped and smoked, and then at last, sighing sadly, he said, My white horse which was stolen last month is still gone. I cannot understand it.

My uncle Khosrove became very irritated and shouted, It's no harm. What is the loss of a horse? Haven't we all lost the homeland? What is this crying over a horse?

That may be all right for you, a city dweller, to say, John Byro said, but what of my surrey? What good is a surrey without a horse?

Pay no attention to it, my uncle Khosrove roared.

I walked ten miles to get here, John Byro said.

You have legs, my uncle Khosrove shouted.

My left leg pains me, the farmer said.

Pay no attention to it, my uncle Khosrove roared.

That horse cost me sixty dollars, the farmer said.

I spit on money, my uncle Khosrove said.

The Beautiful White Horse

He got up and stalked out of the house, slamming the screen door.

My mother explained.

He has a gentle heart, she said. It is simply that he is homesick and such a large man.

The farmer went away and I ran over to my cousin Mourad's house.

He was sitting under a peach tree, trying to repair the hurt wing of a young robin which could not fly. He was talking to the bird.

What is it? he said.

The farmer, John Byro, I said. He visited our house. He wants his horse. You've had it a month. I want you to promise not to take it back until I learn to ride.

It will take you *a year* to learn to ride, my cousin Mourad said.

We could keep the horse a year, I said.

My cousin Mourad leaped to his feet.

What? he roared. Are you inviting a member of the Garoghlanian family to steal? The horse must go back to its true owner.

When? I said.

In six months at the latest, he said.

He threw the bird into the air. The bird tried

hard, almost fell twice, but at last flew away, high and straight.

Early every morning for two weeks my cousin Mourad and I took the horse out of the barn of the deserted vineyard where we were hiding it and rode it, and every morning the horse, when it was my turn to ride alone, leaped over grape vines and small trees and threw me and ran away. Nevertheless, I hoped in time to learn to ride the way my cousin Mourad rode.

One morning on the way to Fetvajian's deserted vineyard we ran into the farmer John Byro who was on his way to town.

Let me do the talking, my cousin Mourad said. I have a way with farmers.

Good morning, John Byro, my cousin Mourad said to the farmer.

The farmer studied the horse eagerly.

Good morning, sons of my friends, he said. What is the name of your horse?

My Heart, my cousin Mourad said in Armenian.

A lovely name, John Byro said, for a lovely horse. I could swear it is the horse that was stolen from me many weeks ago. May I look into its mouth?

14

The Beautiful White Horse

Of course, Mourad said.

The farmer looked into the mouth of the horse.

Tooth for tooth, he said. I would swear it *is* my horse if I didn't know your parents. The fame of your family for honesty is well known to me. Yet the horse is the twin of my horse. A suspicious man would believe his eyes instead of his heart. Good day, my young friends.

Good day, John Byro, my cousin Mourad said.

Early the following morning we took the horse to John Byro's vineyard and put it in the barn. The dogs followed us around without making a sound.

The dogs, I whispered to my cousin Mourad. I thought they would bark.

They would at somebody else, he said. I have a way with dogs.

My cousin Mourad put his arms around the horse, pressed his nose into the horse's nose, patted it, and then we went away.

That afternoon John Byro came to our house in his surrey and showed my mother the horse that had been stolen and returned.

I do not know what to think, he said. The

horse is stronger than ever. Better-tempered, too. I thank God.

My uncle Khosrove, who was in the parlor, became irritated and shouted, Quiet, man, quiet. Your horse has been returned. Pay no attention to it.

THE JOURNEY TO

HANFORD

T HE time came one year for my sad uncle Jorgi to fix his bicycle and ride twenty-seven miles to Hanford, where it seems there was a job. I went with him, although at first there was talk of sending my cousin Vask instead.

The family didn't want to complain about having among its members a fool like Jorgi, but at the same time it wanted a chance, in the summertime, to forget him for a while. If he went away and got himself a job in Hanford, in the watermelons, all would be well. Jorgi would earn a little money and at the same time be out of the way. That was the important thing—to get him out of the way.

To hell with him and his zither both, my grandfather said. When you read in a book that a man sits all day under a tree and plays a zither and sings, believe me, that writer is an impractical man. Money, that's the thing. Let him go and sweat under the sun for a while. Him and his zither both.

You say that now, my grandmother said, but wait a week. Wait till you begin to need music again.

That is nonsense, my grandfather said. When you read in a book that a man who sings is one who is truly a happy man, that writer is a dreamer, not a merchant in a thousand years. Let him go. It is twenty-seven miles to Hanford. That is a good intelligent distance.

You speak that way *now*, my grandmother said, but in three days you'll be a melancholy man. I shall see you walking about like a tiger. I am the one who shall see that. Seeing that, I am the one who shall laugh.

You are a woman, my grandfather said. When you read in a book with hundreds of pages of small print that a woman is truly a creature of wonder, that writer has turned his face from his wife and is dreaming. Let him go.

It is simply that you are not young any longer, my grandmother said. That is the thing that is making you roar.

The Journey to Hanford

Close your mouth, my grandfather said. Close it, or here comes the back of my hand.

My grandfather looked about the room at his children and grandchildren.

I say he goes to Hanford on his bicycle, he said. What do you say?

Nobody spoke.

Then that's settled, my grandfather said. Now, who shall we send with him? Which of the uncouth of our children shall we punish by sending him with Jorgi to Hanford? When you read in a book that a journey to another city is a pleasant experience for a young man, that writer is probably a man of eighty or ninety who as a child once went in a wagon two miles from home. Who shall we punish? Vask? Shall Vask be the one? Step up here, boy.

My cousin Vask got up from the floor and stood in front of the old man, who looked down at him furiously, twisted his enormous mustaches, cleared his throat, and put his hand over the boy's face. His hand practically covered the whole head. Vask didn't move.

Shall you go with your uncle Jorgi to Hanford? my grandfather said.

If it pleases my grandfather, I shall, Vask said.

The old man began to make faces, thinking it over.

Let me think a moment, he said. Jorgi's spirit is the foolish one of our tribe. Yours is also. Is it wise to put two fools together?

He turned to the others.

Let me hear your spoken thoughts on this theme, he said. Is it wise to put a grown fool and a growing one together, of the same tribe? Will it profit anyone? Speak aloud so I may consider.

I think it would be the natural thing to do, my uncle Zorab said. A fool and a fool. The man to work, the boy to keep house and cook.

Perhaps, my grandfather said. Let's consider. A fool and a fool, one to work, the other to keep house and cook. Can you cook, boy?

Of course he can cook, my grandmother said. Rice, at least.

Is that true, boy, about the rice? my grandfather said. Four cups of water, one cup of rice, one teaspoonful of salt. Do you know about the trick of making it come out like food instead of swill, or are we dreaming?

Of course he can cook rice, my grandmother said.

The back of my hand is on its way to your

mouth, my grandfather said. Let the boy speak
for himself. He has a tongue. Can you do it, boy?
When you read in a book that a boy answers an
old man wisely, that writer is probably a Jew,
bent on exaggeration. Can you make it come out
like food, not swill?

I have cooked rice, Vask said. It came out like
food.

Was there enough salt to it? my grandfather
said. If you lie, remember my hand.

Vask hesitated a moment.

I understand, my grandfather said. You are embarrassed about the rice. What was wrong with it?
Truth is all that pleases me. Speak up fearlessly.
If it is the truth fearlessly, no man can demand
more. What embarrasses you about the rice?

It was too salty, Vask said. We had to drink
water all day and all night, it was so salty.

No elaboration, my grandfather said. Only
what is true. The rice was too salty. Naturally you
had to drink water all day and all night. We've
all eaten that kind of rice. Don't think because
you drank water all day and all night that you are
the first Armenian who ever did that. Just tell me
that it was too salty. I'm not here to learn. I *know*.

Just say it was too salty and let me try to determine if you are the one to go.

My grandfather turned to the others. He began to make faces again.

I think this is the boy to go, he said, but speak up, if you have something to say. Salty is better than swill. Was it light in texture, boy?

It was light in texture, Vask said.

I believe this is the one to send, my grandfather said. The water is good for the gut. Shall it be this boy, Vask Garoghlanian, or who?

On second thought, my uncle Zorab said, two fools, out and out, perhaps not, although the rice is not swill. I nominate Aram. Perhaps he should go. He deserves to be punished.

Everybody looked at me.

Aram? my grandfather said. You mean the boy who laughs? You mean loud-laughing Aram Garoghlanian?

Who else would he mean? my grandmother said. You know very well who he means.

My grandfather turned slowly and for half a minute looked at my grandmother.

When you read in a book, he said, about some man who falls in love with a girl and marries her, that writer is truly referring to a very young man who has no idea she is going to talk out of turn right up to the time she is ready to go into the ground at the age of ninety-seven. That writer is thinking of a younger type of man.

Do you mean Aram? he said. Aram Garoghlanian?

Yes, my uncle Zorab said.

What has he done to deserve this awful punishment? my grandfather said.

He knows, my uncle Zorab said.

Aram Garoghlanian, my grandfather said.

I got up and stood in front of my grandfather. He put his big hand over my face and rubbed it. I knew he was not angry.

What have you done, boy? he said.

I began to laugh, remembering the things I had done. My grandfather listened a moment and then began laughing with me.

Only he and I laughed. The others didn't dare laugh. My grandfather had instructed them not to laugh unless they could laugh like him. I was the only other Garoghlanian in the world who laughed that way.

Aram Garoghlanian, my grandfather said, tell me. What have you done?

Which one? I said.

My grandfather turned to my uncle Zorab.

Which one? he said. Tell the boy which mischief to acknowledge. There appear to be several.

He knows which one, my uncle Zorab said.

Do you mean, I said, telling the neighbors you are crazy?

My uncle Zorab refused to speak.

Or do you mean, I said, going around talking the way you talk?

This is the boy to send with Jorgi, my uncle Zorab said.

Can you cook rice? my grandfather said.

He didn't care to go into detail about my making fun of my uncle Zorab. If I could cook rice, I should go with Jorgi to Hanford. That was what it came to. Of course I *wanted* to go, no matter what the writer was who wrote that it was a fine experience for a boy to travel. Fool or liar or anything else, I *wanted* to go.

I can cook rice, I said.

Salty or swill, or what? my grandfather said.

Sometimes salty, I said. Sometimes swill. Sometimes perfect.

Let's consider, my grandfather said.

He leaned against the wall, considering.

The Journey to Hanford

Three large glasses of water, he said to my grandmother.

My grandmother went to the kitchen and after a moment returned with three large glasses of water on a tray. My grandfather drank one glass after another, then turned to the others, making many thoughtful faces.

Sometimes salty, he said. Sometimes swill. Sometimes perfect. Is this the boy to send to Hanford?

Yes, my uncle Zorab said. The only one.

So be it, my grandfather said. That will be all. I wish to be alone.

I moved to go. My grandfather took me by the neck.

Stay a moment, he said.

When we were alone he said, Talk the way your uncle Zorab talks.

I did so and my grandfather roared with laughter.

Go to Hanford, he said. Go with the fool Jorgi and make it salty or make it swill or make it perfect.

In this manner I was assigned to be my uncle Jorgi's companion on his journey to Hanford.

We set out the following morning before daybreak. I sat on the crossbar of the bicycle and my uncle Jorgi on the seat, but when I got tired I got off and walked, and after a while my uncle Jorgi got off and walked, and I rode. We didn't reach Hanford till late that afternoon.

We were supposed to stay in Hanford till the job ended, after the watermelon season. That was the idea. We went around town looking for a house to stay in, a house with a stove in it, gas connections, and water. We didn't care about electricity, but we wanted gas and water. We saw six or seven houses and then we saw one my uncle Jorgi liked, so we moved in that night. It was an eleven-room house, with a gas stove, a sink with running water, and a room with a bed and a couch. The other rooms were all empty. My uncle Jorgi lighted a candle, brought out his zither, sat on the floor, and began to play and sing. It was beautiful. It was melancholy sometimes and sometimes funny, but it was always beautiful. I don't know how long he played and sang before he realized he was hungry, but all of a sudden he got up off the floor and said, Aram, I want rice.

I made a pot of rice that night that was both salty and swill, but my uncle Jorgi said, Aram, this is wonderful.

The Journey to Hanford

The birds got us up at daybreak.

The job, I said. You begin today, you know.

Today, my uncle Jorgi groaned.

He walked tragically out of the empty house and I looked around for a broom. There was no broom, so I went out and sat on the steps of the front porch. It seemed to be a nice region of the world in daylight. It was a street with only four houses. There was a church steeple in front of the house, two blocks away. I sat on the porch about an hour. My uncle Jorgi came up the street, on his bicycle, zigzagging with joy unconfined.

Not this year, thank God, he said.

He fell off his bicycle into a rose bush.

What? I said.

There is no job, he said. No job, thank God.

He smelled a rose.

No job? I said.

No job, thank our Heavenly Father, he said.

He looked at the rose, smiling.

Why not? I said.

The watermelons, he said.

What about them? I said.

The season is over, he said.

That isn't true, I said.

The season is over, my uncle Jorgi said. Believe me, it is over.

Your father will break your head, I said.

The season is over, he said. Praise God, the watermelons are all harvested.

Who said so? I said.

The farmer himself. The farmer himself said so, my uncle Jorgi said.

He just said that, I said. He didn't want to hurt your feelings. He just said that because he knew your heart wouldn't be in your work.

Praise God, my uncle Jorgi said, the whole season is over. All the fine, ripe watermelons have been harvested.

What are we going to do? I said. The season is just beginning.

It's ended, he said. We shall dwell in this house a month and then go home. We have paid six dollars rent and we have money enough for rice. We shall dream here a month and then go home.

With no money, I said.

But in good health, he said. Praise God, who ripened them so early this year.

My uncle Jorgi danced into the house to his zither, and before I could decide what to do about him he was playing and singing. It was so beautiful I didn't even get up and try to chase him out of the house. I just sat on the porch and listened.

We stayed in the house a month and then went home. My grandmother was the first to see us.

It's about time you two came home, she said. He's been raging like a tiger. Give me the money.

There is no money, I said.

Did he work? my grandmother said.

No, I said. He played and sang the whole month.

How did your rice turn out? she said.

Sometimes salty, I said. Sometimes swill. Sometimes perfect. But he didn't work.

His father mustn't know, she said. I have money.

She lifted her dress and got some currency out of a pocket in her pants and put it in my hands.

When he comes home, she said, give him this money.

She looked at me a moment, then added: *Aram Garoghlanian.*

I will do as you say, I said.

When my grandfather came home he began to roar.

Home already? he said. Is the season ended so soon? Where is the money he earned?

I gave him the money.

I won't have him singing all day, my grandfather roared. There is a limit to everything. When you read in a book that a father loves a foolish son more than his wise sons, that writer is a bachelor.

In the yard, under the almond tree, my uncle Jorgi began to play and sing. My grandfather came to a dead halt and began to listen. He sat down on the couch, took off his shoes, and began to make faces.

I went into the kitchen to get three or four glasses of water to quench the thirst from last night's rice. When I came back to the parlor the old man was stretched out on the couch, asleep and smiling, and his son Jorgi was singing hallelujah to the universe at the top of his beautiful, melancholy voice.

THE POMEGRANATE

TREES

MY uncle Melik was just about the worst farmer that ever lived. He was too imaginative and poetic for his own good. What he wanted was beauty. He wanted to plant it and see it grow. I myself planted over one hundred pomegranate trees for my uncle one year back there in the good old days of poetry and youth in the world. I drove a John Deere tractor too, and so did my uncle. It was all pure esthetics, not agriculture. My uncle just liked the idea of planting trees and watching them grow.

Only they wouldn't grow. It was on account of the soil. The soil was desert soil. It was dry. My uncle waved at the six hundred and eighty acres of desert he had bought and he said in the most poetic Armenian anybody ever heard, Here in this awful desolation a garden shall flower, fountains of cold water shall bubble out of the earth, and all things of beauty shall come into being.

Yes, sir, I said.

I was the first and only relative to see the land he had bought. He knew I was a poet at heart, and he believed I would understand the magnificent impulse that was driving him to glorious ruin. I did. I knew as well as he that what he had purchased was worthless desert land. It was away over to hell and gone, at the foot of the Sierra Nevada Mountains. It was full of every kind of desert plant that ever sprang out of dry hot earth. It was overrun with prairie dogs, squirrels, horned toads, snakes, and a variety of smaller forms of life. The space over this land knew only the presence of hawks, eagles, and buzzards. It was a region of loneliness, emptiness, truth, and dignity. It was nature at its proudest, dryest, loneliest, and loveliest.

My uncle and I got out of the Ford roadster in the middle of his land and began to walk over the dry earth.

This land, he said, is my land.

He walked slowly, kicking into the dry soil. A horned toad scrambled over the earth at my uncle's feet. My uncle clutched my shoulder and came to a pious halt.

What is that animal? he said.

That little tiny lizard? I said.

That mouse with horns, my uncle said. What is it?

I don't know for sure, I said. We call them horny toads.

The horned toad came to a halt about three feet away and turned its head.

My uncle looked down at the small animal.

Is it poison? he said.

To eat? I said. Or if it bites you?

Either way, my uncle said.

I don't think it's good to eat, I said. I think it's harmless. I've caught many of them. They grow sad in captivity, but never bite. Shall I catch this one?

Please do, my uncle said.

I sneaked up on the horned toad, then sprang on it while my uncle looked on.

Careful, he said. Are you sure it isn't poison?

I've caught many of them, I said.

I took the horned toad to my uncle. He tried not to seem afraid.

A lovely little thing, isn't it? he said. His voice was unsteady.

Would you like to hold it? I said.

No, my uncle said. You hold it. I have never before been so close to such a thing as this. I see it has eyes. I suppose it can see us.

I suppose it can, I said. It's looking up at you now.

My uncle looked the horned toad straight in the eye. The horned toad looked my uncle straight in the eye. For fully half a minute they looked one another straight in the eye and then the horned toad turned its head aside and looked down at the ground. My uncle sighed with relief.

A thousand of them, he said, could kill a man, I suppose.

They never travel in great numbers, I said. You hardly ever see more than one at a time.

A big one, my uncle said, could probably bite a man to death.

They don't grow big, I said. This is as big as they grow.

They seem to have an awful eye for such small creatures, my uncle said. Are you sure they don't mind being picked up?

I suppose they forget all about it the minute you put them down, I said.

Do you really think so? my uncle said.

38

I don't think they have very good memories, I
said.

My uncle straightened up, breathing deeply.

Put the little creature down, he said. Let us not
be cruel to the innocent creations of Almighty
God. If it is not poison and grows no larger than
a mouse and does not travel in great numbers and
has no memory to speak of, let the timid little
thing return to the earth. Let us be gentle toward
these small things which live on the earth with us.

Yes, sir, I said.

I placed the horned toad on the ground.

Gently now, my uncle said. Let no harm come
to this strange dweller on my land.

The horned toad scrambled away.

These little things, I said, have been living on
soil of this kind for centuries.

Centuries? my uncle said. Are you sure?

I'm not sure, I said, but I imagine they have.
They're still here, anyway.

My uncle looked around at his land, at the
cactus and brush growing out of it, at the sky
overhead.

What have they been eating all this time? he
shouted.

I don't know, I said.

What would you say they've been eating? he said.

Insects, I guess.

Insects? my uncle shouted. What sort of insects?

Little bugs, most likely, I said. I don't know their names. I can find out tomorrow at school.

We continued to walk over the dry land. When we came to some holes in the earth my uncle stood over them and said, What lives down there?

Prairie dogs, I said.

What are *they?* he said.

Well, I said, they're something like rats. They belong to the rodent family.

What are all these things doing on my land? my uncle said.

They don't know it's your land, I said. They've been living here a long while.

I don't suppose that horny toad ever looked a man in the eye before, my uncle said.

I don't think so, I said.

Do you think I scared it or anything? my uncle said.

I don't know for sure, I said.

If I did, my uncle said, I didn't mean to. I'm going to build a house here some day.

I didn't know that, I said.

Of course, my uncle said. I'm going to build a magnificent house.

It's pretty far away, I said.

It's only an hour from town, my uncle said.

If you go fifty miles an hour, I said.

It's not fifty miles to town, my uncle said. It's thirty-seven.

Well, you've got to take a little time out for rough roads, I said.

I'll build me the finest house in the world, my uncle said. What else lives on this land?

Well, I said, there are three or four kinds of snakes.

Poison or non-poison? my uncle said.

Mostly non-poison, I said. The rattlesnake is poison, though.

Do you mean to tell me there are *rattlesnakes* on this land? my uncle said.

This is the kind of land rattlesnakes usually live on, I said.

How many? my uncle said.

Per acre? I said. Or on the whole six hundred and eighty acres?

Per acre, my uncle said.

Well, I said, I'd say there are about three per acre, conservatively.

Three per acre? my uncle shouted. Conservatively?

Maybe only two, I said.

How many is that to the whole place? my uncle said.

Well, let's see, I said. Two per acre. Six hundred and eighty acres. About fifteen hundred of them.

Fifteen hundred of them? my uncle said.

An acre is pretty big, I said. Two rattlesnakes per acre isn't many. You don't often see them.

What else have we got around here that's poison? my uncle said.

I don't know of anything else, I said. All the other things are harmless. The rattlesnakes are pretty harmless too, unless you step on them.

All right, my uncle said. You walk ahead and watch where you're going. If you see a rattlesnake, don't step on it. I don't want you to die at the age of eleven.

Yes, sir, I said. I'll watch carefully.

We turned around and walked back to the Ford. I didn't see any rattlesnakes on the way back. We got into the car and my uncle lighted a cigarette.

I'm going to make a garden of this awful desolation, he said.

Yes, sir, I said.

I know what my problems are, my uncle said, and I know how to solve them.

How? I said.

Do you mean the horny toads or the rattlesnakes? my uncle said.

I mean the problems, I said.

Well, my uncle said, the first thing I'm going to do is hire some Mexicans and put them to work.

Doing what? I said.

Clearing the land, my uncle said. Then I'm going to have them dig for water.

Dig where? I said.

Straight down, my uncle said. After we get water, I'm going to have them plow the land and then I'm going to plant.

What are you going to plant? I said. Wheat?

Wheat? my uncle shouted. What do I want with wheat? Bread is five cents a loaf. I'm going to plant pomegranate trees.

How much are pomegranates? I said.

Pomegranates, my uncle said, are practically unknown in this country.

Is that all you're going to plant? I said.

I have in mind, my uncle said, planting several other kinds of trees.

Peach trees? I said.

About ten acres, my uncle said.

How about apricots? I said.

By all means, my uncle said. The apricot is a lovely fruit. Lovely in shape, with a glorious flavor and a most delightful pit. I shall plant about twenty acres of apricot trees.

I hope the Mexicans don't have any trouble finding water, I said. Is there water under this land?

Of course, my uncle said. The important thing is to get started. I shall instruct the men to watch out for rattlesnakes. Pomegranates, he said. Peaches. Apricots. What else?

Figs? I said.

Thirty acres of figs, my uncle said.

How about mulberries? I said. The mulberry tree is a very nice-looking tree.

Mulberries, my uncle said. He moved his tongue around in his mouth. A nice tree, he said.

The Pomegranate Trees

A tree I knew well in the old country. How many acres would you suggest?

About ten, I said.

All right, he said. What else?

Olive trees are nice, I said.

Yes, they are, my uncle said. One of the nicest. About ten acres of olive trees. What else?

Well, I said, I don't suppose apple trees would grow on this kind of land.

I suppose not, my uncle said. I don't like apples anyway.

He started the car and we drove off the dry land on to the dry road. The car bounced about slowly until we reached the road and then we began to travel at a higher rate of speed.

One thing, my uncle said. When we get home I would rather you didn't mention this *farm* to the folks.

Yes, sir, I said. (*Farm?* I thought. *What farm?*)

I want to surprise them, my uncle said. You know how your grandmother is. I'll go ahead with my plans and when everything is in order I'll take the whole family out to the farm and surprise them.

Yes, sir, I said.

Not a word to a living soul, my uncle said.

Yes, sir, I said.

Well, the Mexicans went to work and cleared the land. They cleared about ten acres of it in about two months. There were seven of them. They worked with shovels and hoes. They didn't understand anything about anything. It all seemed very strange, but they never complained. They were being paid and that was the thing that counted. They were two brothers and their sons. One day the older brother, Diego, very politely asked my uncle what it was they were supposed to be doing.

Señor, he said, please forgive me. Why are we cutting down the cactus?

I'm going to farm this land, my uncle said.

The other Mexicans asked Diego in Mexican what my uncle had said and Diego told them.

They didn't believe it was worth the trouble to tell my uncle he couldn't do it. They just went on cutting down the cactus.

The cactus, however, stayed down only for a short while. The land which had been first cleared was already rich again with fresh cactus and brush. My uncle made this observation with considerable amazement.

The Pomegranate Trees

It takes deep plowing to get rid of cactus, I said. You've got to plow it out.

My uncle talked the matter over with Ryan, who had a farm-implement business. Ryan told him not to fool with horses. The modern thing to do was to turn a good tractor loose on the land and do a year's work in a day.

So my uncle bought a John Deere tractor. It was beautiful. A mechanic from Ryan's taught Diego how to operate the tractor, and the next day when my uncle and I reached the land we could see the tractor away out in the desolation and we could hear it booming in the awful emptiness of the desert. It sounded pretty awful. It *was* awful. My uncle thought it was wonderful.

Progress, he said. There's the modern age for you. Ten thousand years ago, he said, it would have taken a hundred men a week to do what the tractor's done today.

Ten thousand years ago? I said. You mean yesterday.

Anyway, my uncle said, there's nothing like these modern conveniences.

The tractor isn't a convenience, I said.

What is it, then? my uncle said. Doesn't the driver sit?

He couldn't very well stand, I said.

Any time they let you sit, my uncle said, it's a convenience. Can you whistle?

Yes, sir, I said. What sort of a song would you like to hear?

Song? my uncle said. I don't want to hear any song. I want you to whistle at that Mexican on the tractor.

What for? I said.

Never mind what for, my uncle said. Just whistle. I want him to know we are here and that we are pleased with his work. He's probably plowed twenty acres.

Yes, sir, I said.

I put the second and third fingers of each hand into my mouth and blew with all my might. It was good and loud. Nevertheless, it didn't seem as if Diego had heard me. He was pretty far away. We were walking toward him anyway, so I couldn't figure out why my uncle wanted me to whistle at him.

Once again, he said.

I whistled once again, but Diego didn't hear.

Louder, my uncle said.

This next time I gave it all I had, and my uncle

48

put his hands over his ears. My face got very red, too. The Mexican on the tractor heard the whistle this time. He slowed the tractor down, turned it around, and began plowing straight across the field toward us.

Do you want him to do that? I said.

It doesn't matter, my uncle said.

In less than a minute and a half the tractor and the Mexican arrived. The Mexican seemed very delighted. He wiped dirt and perspiration off his face and got down from the tractor.

Señor, he said, this is wonderful.

I'm glad you like it, my uncle said.

Would you like a ride? the Mexican asked my uncle.

My uncle didn't know for sure. He looked at me.

Go ahead, he said. Hop on. Have a little ride.

Diego got on the tractor and helped me on. He sat on the metal seat and I stood behind him, holding him. The tractor began to shake, then jumped, and then began to move. It moved swiftly and made a good deal of noise. The Mexican drove around in a big circle and brought the tractor back to my uncle. I jumped off.

49

All right, my uncle said to the Mexican. Go back to your work.

The Mexican drove the tractor back to where he was plowing.

My uncle didn't get water out of the land until many months later. He had wells dug all over the place, but no water came out of the wells. Of course he had motor pumps too, but even then no water came out. A water specialist named Roy came out from Texas with his two younger brothers and they began investigating the land. They told my uncle they'd get water for him. It took them three months and the water was muddy and there wasn't much of it. There was a trickle of muddy water. The specialist told my uncle matters would improve with time and went back to Texas.

Now half the land was cleared and plowed and there was water, so the time had come to plant.

We planted pomegranate trees. They were of the finest quality and very expensive. We planted about seven hundred of them. I myself planted a hundred. My uncle planted quite a few. We had a twenty-acre orchard of pomegranate trees away over to hell and gone in the strangest desolation anybody ever saw. It was the loveliest-looking absurdity imaginable and my uncle was crazy about it. The only trouble was, his money was giving out. Instead of going ahead and trying to make a garden of the whole six hundred and eighty acres, he decided to devote all his time and energy and money to the pomegranate trees.

Only for the time being, he said. Until we begin to market the pomegranates and get our money back.

Yes, sir, I said.

I didn't know for sure, but I figured we wouldn't be getting any pomegranates to speak of off those little trees for two or three years at least, but I didn't say anything. My uncle got rid of the Mexican workers and he and I took over the farm. We had the tractor and a lot of land, so every now and then we drove out to the farm and drove the tractor around, plowing up cactus and turning over the soil between the pomegranate trees. This went on for three years.

One of these days, my uncle said, you'll see the loveliest garden in the world in this desert.

The water situation didn't improve with time, either. Every once in a while there would be a sudden generous spurt of water containing only a few pebbles and my uncle would be greatly pleased, but the next day it would be muddy again and there would be only a little trickle. The pomegranate trees fought bravely for life, but they never did get enough water to come out with any fruit.

There were blossoms after the fourth year. This was a great triumph for my uncle. He went out of his head with joy when he saw them.

Nothing much ever came of the blossoms, though. They were very beautiful, but that was about all. Purple and lonely.

That year my uncle harvested three small pomegranates.

I ate one, he ate one, and we kept the other one up in his office.

The following year I was fifteen. A lot of wonderful things had happened to me. I mean, I had read a number of good writers and I'd grown as tall as my uncle. The farm was still our secret. It had cost my uncle a lot of money, but he was always under the impression that very soon he was going to start marketing his pomegranates and get his money back and go on with his plan to make a garden in the desert.

The Pomegranate Trees

The trees didn't fare very well. They grew a little, but it was hardly noticeable. Quite a few of them withered and died.

That's average, my uncle said. Twenty trees to an acre is only average. We won't plant new trees just now. We'll do that later.

He was still paying for the land, too.

The following year he harvested about two hundred pomegranates. He and I did the harvesting. They were pretty sad-looking pomegranates. We packed them in nice-looking boxes and my uncle shipped them to a wholesale produce house in Chicago. There were eleven boxes.

We didn't hear from the wholesale produce house for a month, so one night my uncle made a long-distance phone call. The produce man, D'Agostino, told my uncle nobody wanted pomegranates.

How much are you asking per box? my uncle shouted over the phone.

One dollar, D'Agostino shouted back.

That's not enough, my uncle shouted. I won't take a nickel less than five dollars a box.

They don't want them at one dollar a box, D'Agostino shouted.

Why not? my uncle shouted.

They don't know what they are, D'Agostino shouted.

What kind of a business man are you anyway? my uncle shouted. They're pomegranates. I want five dollars a box.

I can't sell them, the produce man shouted. I ate one myself and I don't see anything so wonderful about them.

You're crazy, my uncle shouted. There is no other fruit in the world like the pomegranate. Five dollars a box isn't half enough.

What shall I do with them? D'Agostino shouted. I can't sell them. I don't want them.

I see, my uncle whispered. Ship them back. Ship them back express collect.

The phone call cost my uncle about seventeen dollars.

So the eleven boxes came back.

My uncle and I ate most of the pomegranates.

The following year my uncle couldn't make any more payments on the land. He gave the papers back to the man who had sold him the land. I was in the office at the time.

Mr. Griffith, my uncle said, I've got to give you back your property, but I would like to ask a little favor. I've planted twenty acres of pomegranate trees out there on that land and I'd appreciate it very much if you'd let me take care of those trees.

Take care of them? Mr. Griffith said. What in the world for?

My uncle tried to explain, but couldn't. It was too much to try to explain to a man who wasn't sympathetic.

So my uncle lost the land, and the trees, too.

About three years later he and I drove out to the land and walked out to the pomegranate orchard. The trees were all dead. The soil was heavy again with cactus and desert brush. Except for the small dead pomegranate trees the place was exactly the way it had been all the years of the world.

We walked around in the orchard for a while and then went back to the car.

We got into the car and drove back to town.

We didn't say anything because there was such an awful lot to say, and no language to say it in.

ONE OF OUR FUTURE

POETS, YOU MIGHT SAY

WHEN I was the fourteenth brightest pupil in the class of fifteen third-graders at Emerson School, the Board of Education took a day off one day to think things over.

This was years ago.

I was eight going on nine or at the most nine going on ten, and good-natured.

In those days the average Board of Education didn't make a fuss over the children of a small town and if some of the children seemed to be doltish, the average Board of Education assumed that this was natural and let it go at that.

Certain Presbyterian ministers, however, sometimes looked into a sea of young faces and said: You are the future leaders of America, the future captains of industry, the future statesmen, and, I might say, the future poets. This sort of talk always pleased me because I liked to imagine

what sort of future captains of industry pals of
mine like Jimmy Volta and Frankie Sousa were
going to make.

I knew these boys.

They were great baseball players, but by nature idiots, or, in more scientific terminology,
high-grade cretins: healthy, strong, and spirited.
I didn't think they would be apt to develop into
captains of industry and neither did they. If they
were asked what career they intended to shape for
themselves, they would honestly say, I don't
know. Nothing, I guess.

Ordinarily, however, our Board of Education
had no such glorious faith as this in the young
hoodlums it was trying to teach to read and write.

Nevertheless, one day our Board of Education
took a day off to think things over quietly and
after seven hours of steady thinking decided to
put every public school pupil through a thorough
physical examination to solve, if possible, the
mystery of health in the young inhabitants of the
slums.

According to documentary proof, published
and tabulated, all the inhabitants of my neighborhood should have had badly shaped heads,
sunken chests, faulty bone structure, hollow

voices, no energy, distemper, and six or seven other minor organic defects.

According to the evidence before each public school teacher, however, these ruffians from the slums had well-shaped heads, sound chests, handsome figures, loud voices, too much energy, and a continuous compulsion to behave mischievously.

Something was wrong somewhere.

Our Board of Education decided to try to find out what.

They *did* find out.

They found out that the published and tabulated documentary proof was wrong.

It was at this time that I first learned with joy and fury that I was a poet. I remember being in the Civic Auditorium of my home town at high noon with six hundred other future statesmen, and I remember hearing my name sung out by old Miss Ogilvie in a clear hysterical soprano.

The time had arrived for me to climb the seventeen steps to the stage, walk to the center of the stage, strip to the waist, inhale, exhale, and be measured all over.

There was a moment of confusion and indecision, followed quickly by a superhuman impulse to behave with style, which I did, to the horror and bewilderment of the whole Board of Education, three elderly doctors, a half-dozen registered nurses, and six hundred future captains of industry.

Instead of climbing the seventeen steps to the stage, I *leaped*.

I remember old Miss Ogilvie turning to Mr. Rickenbacker, Superintendent of Public Schools, and whispering fearfully: This is Garoghlanian— one of our future poets, I might say.

Mr. Rickenbacker took one quick look at me and said: Oh, I see. Who's he sore at?

Society, old Miss Ogilvie said.

Oh, I see, Mr. Rickenbacker said. So am I, but I'll be damned if I can jump like that. Let's say no more about it.

I flung off my shirt and stood stripped to the waist, a good deal of hair bristling on my chest.

You see? Miss Ogilvie said. A writer.

Inhale, Mr. Rickenbacker said.

For how long? I asked.

As long as possible, Mr. Rickenbacker said.

I began to inhale. Four minutes later I was still doing so. Naturally, the examining staff was a little amazed. They called a speedy meeting while I continued to inhale. After two minutes of heated debate the staff decided to ask me to stop inhaling. Miss Ogilvie explained that unless they *asked* me to stop I would be apt to go on inhaling all afternoon.

That will be enough for the present, Mr. Rickenbacker said.

Already? I said. I'm not even started.

Now exhale, he said.

For how long? I said.

My God! Mr. Rickenbacker said.

You'd better tell him, Miss Ogilvie said. Otherwise he'll exhale all afternoon.

Three or four minutes, Mr. Rickenbacker said.

I exhaled four minutes and was then asked to put on my shirt and go away.

How are things? I asked the staff. Am I in pretty good shape?

Let's say no more about it, Mr. Rickenbacker said. Please go away.

The following year our Board of Education decided to give no more physical examinations. The examinations went along all right as far as future captains of industry were concerned, and future statesmen, but when it came to future poets the examinations ran helter-skelter and amuck, and nobody knew what to do or think.

THE FIFTY-YARD DASH

AFTER a certain letter came to me from New York the year I was twelve, I made up my mind to become the most powerful man in my neighborhood. The letter was from my friend Lionel Strongfort. I had clipped a coupon from *Argosy All-Story Magazine,* signed it, placed it in an envelope, and mailed it to him. He had written back promptly, with an enthusiasm bordering on pure delight, saying I was undoubtedly a man of uncommon intelligence, potentially a giant, and—unlike the average run-of-the-mill people of the world who were, in a manner of speaking, dreamwalkers and daydreamers—a person who would some day be somebody.

His opinion of me was very much like my own. It was pleasant, however, to have the opinion so emphatically corroborated, particularly by a man in New York—and a man with the greatest chest

expansion in the world. With the letter came several photographic reproductions of Mr. Strongfort wearing nothing but a little bit of leopard
skin. He was a tremendous man and claimed that
at one time he had been puny. He was loaded all
over with muscle and appeared to be somebody
who could lift a 1920 Ford roadster and tip it
over.

It was an honor to have him for a friend.

The only trouble was—I didn't have the money.
I forget how much the exact figure was at the
beginning of our acquaintanceship, but I haven't
forgotten that it was an amount completely out
of the question. While I was eager to be grateful
to Mr. Strongfort for his enthusiasm, I didn't
seem to be able to find words with which to explain about not having the money, without immediately appearing to be a dreamwalker and a
daydreamer myself. So, while waiting from one
day to another, looking everywhere for words that
would not blight our friendship and degrade me
to commonness, I talked the matter over with my
uncle Gyko, who was studying Oriental philos-
ophy at the time. He was amazed at my curious
ambition, but quite pleased. He said the secret of
greatness, according to Yoga, was the releasing

within one's self of those mysterious vital forces which are in all men.

These strength, he said in English which he liked to affect when speaking to me, ease from God. I tell you, Aram, eat ease wonderful.

I told him I couldn't begin to become the powerful man I had decided to become until I sent Mr. Strongfort some money.

Mohney! my uncle said with contempt. I tell you, Aram, mohney is nawthing. You cannot bribe God.

Although my uncle Gyko wasn't exactly a puny man, he was certainly not the man Lionel Strongfort was. In a wrestling match I felt certain Mr. Strongfort would get a headlock or a half-nelson or a toe hold on my uncle and either make him give up or squeeze him to death. And then again, on the other hand, I wondered. My uncle was nowhere near as big as Mr. Strongfort, but neither was Mr. Strongfort as dynamically furious as my uncle. It seemed to me that, at best, Mr. Strongfort, in a match with my uncle, would have a great deal of unfamiliar trouble—I mean with the mysterious vital forces that were always getting released in my uncle, so that very often a swift glance from him would make a big man quail and turn away, or, if he had been speaking, stop quickly.

Long before I had discovered words with which to explain to Mr. Strongfort about the money, another letter came from him. It was as cordial as the first, and as a matter of fact, if anything, a little more cordial. I was delighted and ran about, releasing mysterious vital forces, turning handsprings, scrambling up trees, turning somersaults, trying to tip over 1920 Ford roadsters, challenging all comers to wrestle, and in many other ways alarming my relatives and irritating the neighbors.

Not only was Mr. Strongfort not sore at me, he had reduced the cost of the course. Even so, the money necessary was still more than I could get hold of. I was selling papers every day, but *that* money was for bread and stuff like that. For a while I got up very early every morning and went around town looking for a small satchel full of money. During six days of this adventuring I found a nickel and two pennies. I found also a woman's purse containing several foul-smelling cosmetic items, no money, and a slip of paper on which was written in an ignorant hand: Steve Hertwig, 3764 Ventura Avenue.

The Fifty-Yard Dash

Three days after the arrival of Mr. Strongfort's second letter, his third letter came. From this time on our correspondence became one-sided. In fact, I didn't write at all. Mr. Strongfort's communications were overpowering and not at all easy to answer, without money. There was, in fact, almost nothing to say.

It was wintertime when the first letter came, and it was then that I made up my mind to become the most powerful man in my neighborhood and ultimately, for all I knew, one of the most powerful men in the world. I had ideas of my own as to how to go about getting that way, but I had also the warm friendship and high regard of Mr. Strongfort in New York, and the mystical and furious guardianship of my uncle Gyko, at home.

The letters from Mr. Strongfort continued to arrive every two or three days all winter and on into springtime. I remember, the day apricots were ripe enough to steal, the arrival of a most charming letter from my friend in New York. It was a hymn to newness on earth, the arrival of springtime, the time of youth in the heart, of renewal, fresh strength, fresh determination, and many other things. It was truly a beautiful epistle, probably as fine as any to the Romans or anybody else. It was full of the legend-quality, the world-feeling, and the dignity-of-strength-feeling so characteristic of Biblical days. The last paragraph of the lovely hymn brought up, apologetically, the coarse theme of money. The sum was six or seven times as little as it had been originally, and a new element had come into Mr. Strongfort's program of changing me over from a nobody to a giant of tremendous strength, and extreme attractiveness to women. Mr. Strongfort had decided, he said, to teach me everything in one fell swoop, or one sweep fall, or something of that sort. At any rate, for three dollars, he said, he would send me all his precious secrets in one envelope and the rest would be up to me, and history.

I took the matter up with my uncle Gyko, who by this time had reached the stage of fasting, meditating, walking for hours, and vibrating. We had had discussions two or three times a week all winter and he had told me in his own unique broken-English way all the secrets *he* had been learning from Yoga.

I tell you, Aram, he said, I can do *anything*. Eat ease wonderful.

I believed him, too, even though he had lost a

lot of weight, couldn't sleep, and had a strange dynamic blaze in his eyes. He was very scornful of the world that year and was full of pity for the dumb beautiful animals that man was mistreating, killing, eating, domesticating, and teaching to do tricks.

I tell you, Aram, he said, eat ease creaminal to make the horses work. To keal the cows. To teach the dogs to jump, and the monkeys to smoke pipes.

I told him about the letter from Mr. Strongfort.

Mohney! he said. Always he wants mohney. I do not like heem.

My uncle was getting all his dope free from the theosophy-philosophy-astrology-and-miscellaneous shelf at the Public Library. He believed, however, that he was getting it straight from God. Before he took up Yoga he had been one of the boys around town and a good drinker of *rakhi,* but after the light began to come to him he gave up drinking. He said he was drinking liquor finer than *rakhi* or anything else.

What's that? I asked him.

Aram, he said, eat ease weasdom.

73

Anyhow, he had little use for Mr. Strongfort and regarded the man as a charlatan.

He's all right, I told my uncle.

But my uncle became furious, releasing mysterious vital forces, and said, I wheel break hease head, fooling all you leatle keads.

He ain't fooling, I said. He says he'll give me all his secrets for three dollars.

I tell you, Aram, my uncle Gyko said, he does not know any seacrets. He ease a liar.

I don't know, I said. I'd like to try that stuff out.

Eat ease creaminal, my uncle Gyko said, but I wheel geave you tree dollar.

My uncle Gyko gave me the necessary three dollars and I sent them along to Mr. Strongfort. The envelope came from New York, full of Mr. Strongfort's secrets. They were strangely simple. It was all stuff I had known anyhow but had been too lazy to pay any attention to. The idea was to get up early in the morning and for an hour or so to do various kinds of acrobatic exercises, which were illustrated. Also to drink plenty of water, get plenty of fresh air, eat good wholesome food, and keep it up until you were a giant.

I felt a little let down and sent Mr. Strongfort

a short polite note saying so. He ignored the note and I never heard from him again. In the meantime, I had been following the rules and growing more powerful every day. When I say *in the meantime,* I mean for four days I followed the rules. On the fifth day I decided to sleep instead of getting up and filling the house with noise and getting my grandmother sore. She used to wake up in the darkness of early morning and shout that I was an impractical fool and would never be rich. She would go back to sleep for five minutes, wake up, and then shout that I would never buy and sell for a profit. She would sleep a little more, waken, and shout that there were once three sons of a king; one was wise like his father; the other was crazy about girls; and the third had less brains than a bird. Then she would get out of bed, and, shouting steadily, tell me the whole story while I did my exercises.

The story would usually warn me to be sensible and not go around waking her up before daybreak all the time. That would always be the moral, more or less, although the story itself would be about three sons of some king, or three brothers, each of them very wealthy and usually very greedy, or three daughters, or three proverbs, or three roads, or something else like that.

She was wasting her breath, though, because I wasn't enjoying the early-morning acrobatics any more than she was. In fact, I was beginning to feel that it was a lot of nonsense, and that my uncle Gyko had been right about Mr. Strongfort in the first place.

So I gave up Mr. Strongfort's program and returned to my own, which was more or less as follows: to take it easy and grow to be the most powerful man in the neighborhood without any trouble or exercise. Which is what I did.

That spring Longfellow School announced that a track meet was to be held, one school to compete against another; *everybody* to participate.

Here, I believed, was my chance. In my opinion I would be first in every event.

Somehow or other, however, continuous meditation on the theme of athletics had the effect of growing into a fury of anticipation that continued all day and all night, so that before the day of the track meet I had run the fifty-yard dash any number of hundreds of times, had jumped the running broad jump, the standing broad jump, and the high jump, and in each event had made my competitors look like weaklings.

This tremendous inner activity, which was strictly Yoga, changed on the day of the track meet into fever.

The time came at last for me and three other athletes, one of them a Greek, to go to our marks, get set, and go; and I did, in a blind rush of speed which I knew had never before occurred in the history of athletics.

It seemed to me that never before had any living man moved so swiftly. Within myself I ran the fifty yards fifty times before I so much as opened my eyes to find out how far back I had left the other runners. I was very much amazed at what I saw.

Three boys were four yards ahead of me and going away.

It was incredible. It was unbelievable, but it was obviously the truth. There ought to be some mistake, but there wasn't. There they were, ahead of me, going away.

Well, it simply meant that I would have to overtake them, with my eyes open, and win the race. This I proceeded to do. They continued, incredibly, however, to go away, in spite of my intention. I became irritated and decided to put them in their places for the impertinence, and began releasing all the mysterious vital forces within myself that I had. Somehow or other, however, not even this seemed to bring me any closer to them and I felt that in some strange way I was being betrayed. If so, I decided, I would shame my betrayer by winning the race in spite of the betrayal, and once again I threw fresh life and energy into my running. There wasn't a great distance still to go, but I knew I would be able to do it.

Then I knew I wouldn't.

The race was over.

I was last, by ten yards.

Without the slightest hesitation I protested and challenged the runners to another race, same distance, back. They refused to consider the proposal, which proved, I knew, that they were afraid to race me. I told them they knew very well I could beat them.

It was very much the same in all the other events.

When I got home I was in high fever and very angry. I was delirious all night and sick three days. My grandmother took very good care of me and probably was responsible for my not dying. When my uncle Gyko came to visit me he was no longer hollow-cheeked. It seems he had finished his fast, which had been a long one—forty days or so; and nights too, I believe. He had stopped meditating, too, because he had practically exhausted the subject. He was again one of the boys around town, drinking, staying up all hours, and following the women.

I tell you, Aram, he said, we are a great family. We can do *anything*.

A NICE OLD-FASHIONED

ROMANCE, WITH LOVE

LYRICS & EVERYTHING

MY cousin Arak was a year and a half younger than me, round-faced, dark, and exceptionally elegant in manners. It was no pretense with him. His manners were just naturally that way, just as my manners were bad from the beginning. Where Arak would get around any sort of complication at school with a bland smile that showed his front upper teeth, separated, and melted the heart of stone of our teacher, Miss Daffney, I would go to the core of the complication and with noise and vigor prove that Miss Daffney or somebody else was the culprit, not me, and if need be, I would carry the case to the Supreme Court and prove my innocence.

I usually got sent to the office. In some cases I would get a strapping for debating the case in the office against Mr. Derringer, our principal, who was no earthly good at debates. The minute I got him cornered he got out his strap.

Arak was different; he didn't care to fight for justice. He wasn't anywhere near as bright as me, but even though he was a year and a half younger than me, he was in the same grade. That wouldn't be so bad if the grade wasn't the fifth. I usually won all my arguments with my teachers, but instead of being glad to get rid of me they refused to promote me, in the hope, I believe, of winning the following semester's arguments and getting even. That's how it happened that I came to be the oldest pupil in the fifth grade.

One day Miss Daffney tried to tell the world I was the author of the poem on the blackboard that said she was in love with Mr. Derringer, and ugly. The author of the poem was my cousin Arak, not me. Any poem I wrote wouldn't be about Miss Daffney, it would be about something worthwhile. Nevertheless, without mentioning any names, but with a ruler in her hand, Miss Daffney stood beside my desk and said, I am going to find out who is responsible for this horrible outrage on the blackboard and see that he is properly punished.

He? I said. How do you know it's a boy and not a girl?

Miss Daffney whacked me on the knuckles of my right hand. I jumped out of my seat and said, You can't go around whacking me on the knuckles. I'll report this.

Sit down, Miss Daffney said.

I did. She had me by the right ear, which was getting out of shape from being grabbed hold of by Miss Daffney and other teachers.

I sat down and quietly, almost inaudibly, said, You'll hear about this.

Hold your tongue, Miss Daffney said, and although I was sore as the devil, I stuck out my tongue and held it, while the little Mexican, Japanese, Armenian, Greek, Italian, Portuguese, and plain American boys and girls in the class, who looked to me for comedy, roared with laughter. Miss Daffney came down on my hand with the ruler, but this time the ruler grazed my nose. This to me was particularly insulting, inasmuch as my nose then, as now, was large. A small nose would not have been grazed, and I took Miss Daffney's whack as a subtle comment on the size of my nose.

85

I put my bruised hand over my hurt nose and again rose to my feet.

You told me to hold my tongue, I said, insisting that I had done no evil, had merely carried out her instructions, and was therefore innocent, utterly undeserving of the whacked hand and the grazed nose.

You be good now, Miss Daffney said. I won't stand any more of your nonsense. You be good.

I took my hand away from my nose and began to be good. I smiled like a boy bringing her a red apple. My audience roared with laughter and Miss Daffney dropped the ruler, reached for me, fell over the desk, got up, and began to chase me around the room.

There I go again, I kept saying to myself while Miss Daffney chased me around the room. There I go again getting in a mess like this that's sure to end in murder, while my cousin Arak, who is the guilty one, sits there and smiles. There's no justice anywhere.

When Miss Daffney finally caught me, as I knew she would unless I wanted even more severe punishment from Mr. Derringer, there was a sort of free-for-all during which she tried to gouge my eyes out, pull off my ears, fingers, and arms, and

I, by argument, tried to keep her sweet and lady-like.

When she was exhausted, I went back to my seat, and the original crime of the day was taken up again: Who was the author of the love lyric on the blackboard?

Miss Daffney straightened her hair and her clothes, got her breath, demanded and got silence, and after several moments of peace during which the ticking of the clock was heard, she began to speak.

I am going to ask each of you by name if you wrote this awful—poem—on the blackboard and I shall expect you to tell the truth. If you lie, I shall find out anyway and your punishment will be all the worse.

She began to ask each of the boys and girls if they'd written the poem and of course they hadn't. Then she asked my cousin Arak and he also said he hadn't. Then she asked me and I said I hadn't, which was the truth.

You go to the office, she said. You liar.

I didn't write any poem on any blackboard, I said. And I'm not a liar.

Mr. Derringer received me with no delight. Two minutes later Susie Kokomoto arrived from our class with a message describing my crime. In fact, quoting it. Mr. Derringer read the message, made six or seven faces, smiled, snapped his suspenders, coughed and said, What made you write this little poem?

I didn't, I said.

Naturally, he said, you'd say you didn't, but why did you?

I *didn't* write it, I said.

Now don't be headstrong, Mr. Derringer said. That's a rather alarming rumor to be spreading. How do you *know* Miss Daffney's in love with me?

Is she? I said.

Well, Mr. Derringer said, that's what it says here. What gave you that impression? Have you noticed her looking at me with admiration or something?

I haven't noticed her looking at you with anything, I said. Are *you* in love with *her* or something?

That remains to be seen, Mr. Derringer said. It isn't a bad poem, up to a point. Do you really regard Miss Daffney as ugly?

I didn't write the poem, I said. I can prove it. I don't write that way.

You mean your handwriting isn't like the handwriting on the blackboard? Mr. Derringer said.

Yes, I said, and I don't write that kind of poetry either.

You *admit* writing poetry? Mr. Derringer said.

I write poetry, I said, but not *that* kind of poetry.

A rumor like that, Mr. Derringer said. I hope you know what you're about.

Well, I said, all I know is I didn't write it.

Personally, Mr. Derringer said, I think Miss Daffney is not only not ugly, but on the contrary attractive.

Well, that's all right, I said. The only thing I want is not to get into a lot of trouble over something I didn't do.

You *could* have written that poem, Mr. Derringer said.

Not *that* one, I said. I could have written a good one.

What do you mean, *good?* Mr. Derringer said. Beautiful? Or insulting?

I mean beautiful, I said, only it wouldn't be about Miss Daffney.

Up to this point, Mr. Derringer said, I was willing to entertain doubts as to your being the author of the poem, but no longer. I am convinced you wrote it. Therefore I must punish you.

I got up and started to debate.

You give me a strapping for something I didn't do, I said, and you'll hear about it.

So he gave me a strapping and *the whole school* heard about it. I went back to class limping. The poem had been erased. All was well again. The culprit had been duly punished, the poem effaced, and order re-established in the fifth grade. My cousin Arak sat quietly admiring Alice Bovard's brown curls.

First thing during recess I knocked him down and sat on him.

I got a strapping for that, I said, so don't write any more of them.

The next morning, however, there was another love lyric on the blackboard in my cousin Arak's unmistakable hand, and in his unmistakable style, and once again Miss Daffney wanted to weed out the culprit and have him punished. When I came into the room and saw the poem and the lay of the land I immediately began to object. My cousin Arak was going too far. In Armenian I began to swear at him. He, however, had become stone deaf, and Miss Daffney believed my talk was for her. Here, here, she said. Speak in a language everybody can understand if you've got something to say.

All I've got to say is I didn't write that poem, I said. And I didn't write yesterday's either. If I get into any more trouble on account of these poems, somebody's going to hear about it.

Sit down, Miss Daffney said.

After the rollcall, Miss Daffney filled a whole sheet of paper with writing, including the new poem, and ordered me to take the message to the office.

Why *me?* I said. I didn't write the poem.

Do as you're told, Miss Daffney said.

I went to her desk, put out my hand to take the note, Miss Daffney gave it a whack, I jumped back three feet and shouted, I'm not going to be carrying love-letters for you.

This just naturally was the limit. There was a limit to everything. Miss Daffney leaped at me. I in turn was so sore at my cousin Arak that I turned around and jumped on him. He pretended to be very innocent, and offered no resistance. He was very deft, though, and instead of getting the worst of it, he got the least, while I fell all over the floor until Miss Daffney caught up with me.

After that it was all her fight. When I got to the office with the message, I had scratches and bruises all over my face and hands, and the love-letter from Miss Daffney to Mr. Derringer was crumpled and in places torn.

What's been keeping you? Mr. Derringer said. Here, let me see that message. What mischief have you been up to now?

He took the message, unfolded it, smoothed it out on his desk, and read it very slowly. He read it three or four times. He was delighted, and, as far as I could tell, in love. He turned with a huge smile on his face and was about to reprimand me again for saying that Miss Daffney was ugly.

I didn't write the poem, I said. I didn't write yesterday's either. All I want is a chance to get myself a little education and live and let live.

Now, now, Mr. Derringer said.

He was quite pleased.

If you're in love with her, I said, that's your affair, but leave me out of it.

All I say is you could be a little more gracious about Miss Daffney's appearance, Mr. Derringer said. If she seems plain to you, perhaps she doesn't seem plain to someone else.

I was disgusted. It was just no use.

All right, I said. Tomorrow I'll be gracious.

Now that's better, Mr. Derringer said. Of course I must punish you.

He reached for the lower drawer of his desk where the strap was.

Oh, no, I said. If you punish me, then I won't be gracious.

Well, what about today's poem? Mr. Derringer said. I've got to punish you for that. Tomorrow's will be another story.

No, I said. Nothing doing.

Oh, all right, Mr. Derringer said, but see that you're gracious.

I will, I said. Can I go back now?

Yes, he said. Yes. Let me think this over.

I began to leave the office.

Wait a minute, he said. Everybody'll know something fishy's going on somewhere unless they hear you howl. Better come back here and howl ten times, and then go back.

Howl? I said. I can't howl unless I'm hurt.

Oh, sure you can, Mr. Derringer said. Just give out a big painful howl. You can do it.

I don't think I can, I said.

I'll hit this chair ten times with the strap, Mr. Derringer said, and you howl.

Do you think it'll work? I said.

Of course it'll work, he said. Come on.

Mr. Derringer hit the chair with the strap and I tried to howl the way I had howled yesterday, but it didn't sound real. It sounded fishy, somewhere.

We were going along that way when Miss Daffney herself came into the office, only we didn't know she'd come in, on account of the noise.

On the tenth one I turned to Mr. Derringer and said, That's ten.

Then I saw Miss Daffney. She was aghast and mouth-agape.

Just a few more, son, Mr. Derringer said, for good measure.

Before I could tell him Miss Daffney was in the office, he was whacking the chair again and I was howling.

It was disgusting.

Miss Daffney coughed and Mr. Derringer turned and saw her—his beloved.

Miss Daffney didn't speak. She *couldn't*. Mr. Derringer smiled. He was very embarrassed and began swinging the strap around.

I'm punishing the boy, he said.

A Nice Old-Fashioned Romance

I understand, Miss Daffney said.

She didn't either. Not altogether anyway.

I'll not have any pupil of this school being impertinent, Mr. Derringer said.

He was madly in love with her and was swinging the strap around and trying to put over a little personality. Miss Daffney, however, just didn't think very much of his punishing the boy by hitting a chair, while the boy howled, the man and the boy together making a mockery of justice and true love. She gave him a very dirty look.

Oh! Mr. Derringer said. You mean about my hitting the chair? We were just rehearsing, weren't we, son?

No, we weren't, I said.

Miss Daffney, infuriated, turned and fled, and Mr. Derringer sat down.

Now look what you've done, he said.

Well, I said, if you're going to have a romance with her, have it, but don't mess me up in it.

Well, Mr. Derringer said, I guess that's that.

He was a very sad man.

All right, he said, go back to your class.

I want you to know I didn't write them poems, I said.

That's got nothing to do with it, Mr. Derringer said.

I thought you might want to know, I said.

It's too late now, he said. She'll never admire me any more.

Why don't you write a poem to her yourself? I said.

I can't write poems, Mr. Derringer said.

Well, I said, figure it out some way.

When I went back to class Miss Daffney was very polite. So was I. She knew I knew and she knew if she got funny I'd either ruin the romance or make her marry him, so she was very friendly. In two weeks school closed and when school opened again Miss Daffney didn't show up. Either Mr. Derringer didn't write her a poem, or did and it was no good; or he didn't tell her he loved her, or did and she didn't care; or else he proposed to her and she turned him down, *because I knew,* and got herself transferred to another school so she could get over her broken heart.

Something like that.

MY COUSIN DIKRAN,

THE ORATOR

TWENTY years ago, in the San Joaquin Valley, the Armenians used to regard oratory as the greatest, the noblest, the most important, one might say the *only*, art. About ninety-two per cent of the vineyardists around Fresno, by actual count, believed that any man who could make a speech was a cultured man. This was so, I imagine after all these years, because the vineyardists themselves were so ineffective at speechmaking, so self-conscious about it, so embarrassed, and so profoundly impressed by public speakers who could get up on a platform, adjust spectacles on their noses, look at their pocket watches, cough politely, and, beginning quietly, lift their voices to a roar that shook the farmers to the roots and made them know the speaker was educated.

What language! What energy! What wisdom!

99

What magnificent roaring! the farmers said to
themselves.

The farmers, assembled in the basement of one
or another of the three churches, or in the Civic
Auditorium, trembled with awe, wiped the tears
from their eyes, blew their noses, and, momen-
tarily overcome, donated as much money as they
could afford. On some occasions, such as when
money was being raised for some especially inti-
mate cause, the farmers, in donating money,
would stand up in the auditorium and cry out,
Mgerdich Kasabian, his wife Araxie, his three
sons, Gourken, Sirak, and Toumas—fifty cents!
and sit down amid thunderous applause, not so
much for the sum of money donated as for the
magnificent manner of speaking, and the excellent and dramatic pronunciation of the fine old-
country names: Mgerdich, Araxie, Gourken,
Sirak, Toumas.

In this matter of speaking and donating money,
the farmers competed with one another. If a
farmer did not get up and publicly make his an-
nouncement like a man—well, then, the poor fellow! Neither money nor the heart to get up fearlessly and throw away the trembling in his soul!
Because of this competition, a farmer unable to

donate money (but with every impulse in the world to help the cause), would sit nervously in shame year after year, and then finally, with the arrival of better days, leap to his feet, look about the auditorium furiously, and shout, Gone are the days of poverty for this tribe from the lovely city of Dikranagert—the five Pampalonian brothers— twenty-five cents! and go home with his head high, and his heart higher. Poor? In the old days, yes. But no more. (And the five enormous men would look at one another with family pride, and push their sons before them—with affection, of course; that strange Near-Eastern, Oriental affection that came from delight in no longer being humiliated in the eyes of one's countrymen.)

No farmer was prouder, however, than when his son, at school, at church, at a picnic, or any-where, got up and made a speech.

The boy! the farmer would shout at his eighty-eight-year-old father. Listen to him! It's Vahan, my son, *your* grandson—eleven years old. He's talking about Europe.

The grandfather would shake his head and wonder what it was all about, a boy of eleven so serious and so well-informed, talking about Europe. The old man scarcely would know where

Europe was, although he would know he had
visited Havre, in France, on his way to America.
Perhaps Havre—perhaps that was it. *Yevroba.*
Europe. But what in the world could be the matter with Havre suddenly—to make the boy so
tense and excited? Ahkh, the old man would
groan, it is all beyond me. I don't remember. It
was a pleasant city on the sea, with ships.

The women would be overjoyed and full of
amazement at themselves, the mothers. They
would look about at one another, nodding, shak-
ing their heads, and after ten minutes of the boy's
talking in English, which they couldn't understand, they would burst into sweet silent tears because it was all so amazing and wonderful—little
Berjie, only yesterday a baby who couldn't speak
two words of Armenian, let alone English, on a
platform, speaking, swinging his arms, pointing a
finger, now at the ceiling, now west, now south,
now north, and occasionally at his heart.

It was inevitable under these circumstances for
the Garoghlanians to produce an orator too, even
though the Old Man regarded speechmakers as
fools and frauds.

When you hear a small man with spectacles on
his face shouting from the bottom of his bowels,

let me tell you that that man is either a jackass or a liar.

He was always impatient with any kind of talk, except the most direct and pertinent. He wanted to know what he didn't know, and that was all. He wanted no talk for talk's sake. He used to go to all the public meetings, but they never failed to sicken him. Every speaker would watch his face to learn how displeased the Old Man was, and when they saw his lips moving with silent curses they would calm down and try to talk sense, or, if they had talked to him in private and learned how stupid he regarded them, they would try to get even with him by shouting louder than ever and occasionally coming forth with, We know there are those among us who scoff at us, who ridicule our efforts, who even, out of fantastic pride of heart, regard us as fools, but this has always been the cross we have had to carry, and carry it we will.

Here the Old Man would tap his sons on their heads, these in turn would tap their sons on their heads, these would nudge one another, the women would look about, and together the Garogh-lanians, numbering thirty-seven or thirty-eight, would rise and walk out, with the Old Man look-

ing about furiously at the poor farmers and saying, They're carrying the cross again—let's go.

In spite of all this, I say, it was inevitable for
the Garoghlanians to produce an orator. It was
the style, the will of the people, and some member
of the Garoghlanian tribe would naturally find it
essential to enter the field and show everybody
what oratory could really be—what, in fact, it
really was, if the truth were known.

This Garoghlanian turned out to be my little
cousin Dikran, my uncle Zorab's second son, who
was nine years old when the war ended, a year
younger than myself, but so much smaller in size
that I regarded him as somebody to ignore.

From the beginning this boy was one of those
very bright boys who have precious little real understanding, no humor at all, and the disgraceful
and insulting attitude that all knowledge comes
from the outside—disgraceful particularly to the
Garoghlanians, who for centuries had come by all
their wisdom naturally, from within. It was the
boast of the Old Man that any real Garoghlanian
could spot a crook in one glance, and would have
the instinctive good sense to know how to deal
with the man.

When you look at a man who hides behind his

face, the Old Man used to say, let me tell you that that man is no good. He is either a spy or a swindler. On the other hand, if you look at a man whose glance tells you, *Brother, I am your brother*—watch out. That man carries a knife on his person somewhere.

With instruction of this sort, beginning practically at birth, it was only natural for the average Garoghlanian to grow up in wisdom of the world and its strange inhabitants.

The only Garoghlanian who couldn't catch on, however, was this cousin of mine, Dikran. He was strictly a book-reader, a type of human being extremely contemptible to the Old Man, unless he could perceive definite improvement in the character of the reader—of necessity a child, as who else would read a book? In the case of Dikran, the Old Man could perceive no improvement; on the contrary, a continuous decline in understanding, until at last, when the boy was eleven, the Old Man was informed that Dikran was the brightest pupil at Longfellow School, the pride of his teachers, and an accomplished public speaker.

When this news was brought to the Old Man by the boy's mother, the Old Man, who was lying on the couch in the parlor, turned his face to the wall and groaned, Too bad. What a waste. What's eating the boy?

Why, he's the brightest boy in the whole school, the mother said.

The Old Man sat up and said, When you hear of a boy of eleven being the brightest boy in a school of five hundred boys—pay no attention to it. For the love of God, what's he bright about? Isn't he eleven? What bright? Who wants a child to burden himself with such a pathetic sense of importance? You have been a poor mother, I must tell you. Drive the poor boy out of the house into the fields. Let him go swimming with his cousins. The poor fellow doesn't even know how to laugh. And you come here in the afternoon to tell me he is bright. Well, go away.

In spite of even this, I say, the boy moved steadily forward, turning the pages of books day and night, Sundays and holidays and picnic days, until finally, on top of everything else, it was necessary to fit glasses to his face—which made him all the more miserable-looking, so that every time there was a family gathering the Old Man would look about, see the boy, and groan, My God, the philosopher! All right, boy, come here.

The boy would get up and stand in front of the Old Man.

Well, the Old Man would say, you read books. That's fine. You are now eleven years old. Thank God for that. Now tell me—what do you know? What have you learned?

I can't tell you in Armenian, the boy would say.

I see, the Old Man would say. Well, tell me in English.

Here everything would go beautifully haywire. This little cousin of mine, eleven years old, would really begin to make a speech about all the wonderful things he had found out from the books. They *were* wonderful, too. He knew all the dates, all the reasons, all the names, all the places, and what the consequences were likely to be.

It was very beautiful in a minor, melancholy way.

Suddenly the Old Man would stop the boy's speech, shouting, What are you—a parrot?

Even so, it seemed to me that the Old Man was fond of this strange arrival among the Garoghlanians. Book-readers were fools—and so were orators—but at any rate *our* book-reader and orator was not by any means a run-of-the-mill book-reader and orator. He was at any rate something special. For one thing he was younger than the others who imagined they had learned many things from books, and for another he spoke a lot more clearly than the others.

For these reasons, and because of the evident determination in the boy to follow his own inclination, he was accepted by all of us as the Garoghlanian scholar and orator, and permitted to occupy his time and develop whatever mind he may have been born with as he pleased.

In 1920, Longfellow School announced an evening program consisting of (1) Glee Club Singing, (2) a performance of *Julius Caesar,* and (3) a speech by Dikran Garoghlanian—a speech entitled *Was the World War Fought in Vain?* At the proper time the Garoghlanians seated themselves in the school auditorium, listened to the awful singing, watched the horrible performance of *Julius Caesar,* and then listened to the one and only Garoghlanian orator—Dikran, the second son of Zorab.

The speech was flawless: dramatic, well-uttered, intelligent, and terribly convincing—the conclusion being that the World War had *not* been fought in vain, that Democracy *had* saved the world. Everybody in the auditorium was stricken with awe, and applauded the speech wildly. It was really too much, though—I mean for the Old Man. In the midst of the thunderous applause, he burst out laughing. The speech was really splendid, in a way. It was at least the best thing of its kind—the best of the worst kind of thing. There was some occasion for pride in this, even.

That evening at home the Old Man called the boy to him and said, I listened to your speech. It's all right. I understand you spoke about a war in which several million men were killed. I understand you *proved* the war was not fought in vain. I must tell you I am rather pleased. A statement as large and as beautiful as that deserves to come only from the lips of a boy of eleven—from one who believes what he is saying. From a grown man, I must tell you, the horror of that remark would be just a little too much for me to endure. Continue your investigation of the world from books, and I am sure, if you are diligent and your eyes hold out, that by the time you are sixty-seven you will know the awful foolishness of that remark—so innocently uttered by yourself tonight, in such a pure flow of soprano English. In a way I am as proud of you as of any other member of this tribe. You may all go now. I want to sleep. I am not eleven years old. I am sixty-seven.

Everybody got up and went away, except me. I stayed behind long enough to see the old man take off his shoes and hear him sigh, These crazy wonderful children of this crazy wonderful world!

THE PRESBYTERIAN

CHOIR SINGERS

ONE of the many curious and delightful
things about our country is the ease with which
our good people move from one religion to another, or from no particular religion at all to any
religion that happens to come along, without ex-
periencing any particular loss or gain, and go
right on being innocent anyhow.

Myself, I was born, for instance, a kind of
Catholic, although I was not baptized until I
was thirteen, a circumstance which, I remember
clearly, irritated the priest very much and im-
pelled him to ask my people if they were crazy, to
which my people replied, We have been away.

Thirteen years old and not baptized! the priest
shouted. What kind of people are you?

For the most part, my uncle Melik replied, we
are an agricultural people, although we have had
our brilliant men, too.

It was a Saturday afternoon. The whole thing took no more than seven minutes, but even after I was baptized it was impossible for me to feel any change.

Well, my grandmother said, you are now baptized. Do you feel any better?

For some months, I believe I ought to explain, I had been feeling intelligent, which led my grandmother to suspect that I was ill with some mysterious illness or that I was losing my mind.

I think I feel the same, I said.

Do you believe now? she shouted. Or do you still have doubts?

I can easily *say* I believe, I said, but to tell you the truth I don't know for sure. I want to be a Christian of course.

Well, just believe then, my grandmother said, and go about your business.

My business was in some ways quaint and in other ways incredible.

I sang in the Boys Choir at the Presbyterian Church on Tulare Street. For doing so I received one dollar a week from an elderly Christian lady named Balaifal who lived in sorrow and solitude in the small ivy-covered house next to the house in which my friend Pandro Kolkhozian lived.

The Presbyterian Choir Singers

This boy, like myself, was loud in speech. That is to say, we swore a good deal—in all innocence of course—and by doing so grieved Miss or Mrs. Balaifal so much that she sought to save us while there was still time. To be saved was a thing I for one had no occasion to resent.

Miss Balaifal (I shall call her that from now on, since while I knew her she was certainly single, and since I do not know for sure if she ever married, or for that matter if she ever thought of marrying, or if she ever so much as fell in love— earlier in life of course, and no doubt with a scoundrel who took the whole matter with a grain of salt)—Miss Balaifal, as I began to say, was a cultured woman, a reader of the poems of Robert Browning and other poets and a woman of great sensitivity, so that coming out on the porch of her house to hear us talk she could stand so much and no more, and when the limit had been reached, cried out, Boys, boys. You must not use profane language.

Pandro Kolkhozian, on the one hand, seemed to be the most uncouth boy in the world and on the other—and this was the quality in him which endeared him to me—the most courteous and thoughtful.

Yes, Miss Balaifum, he said.

Balaifal, the lady corrected him. Please come here. Both of you.

We went to Miss Balaifal and asked what she wanted.

What do you want, Miss Balaifum? Pandro said.

Miss Balaifal went into her coat pocket and brought out a sheaf of pamphlets, and without looking at them handed one to each of us. My pamphlet was entitled *Redemption, The Story of a Drunkard.* Pandro's was entitled *Peace at Last, The Story of a Drunkard.*

What's this for? Pandro said.

I want you boys to read those pamphlets and try to be good, Miss Balaifal said. I want you to stop using profane language.

It doesn't say anything here about profane language, Pandro said.

There's a good lesson for each of you in those pamphlets, the lady said. Read them and don't use profane language any more.

Yes, ma'am, I said. Is that all?

One thing more, Miss Balaifal said. I wonder if you boys would help me move the organ from the dining room to the parlor?

Sure, Miss Balaifum, Pandro said. Any time.

So we went into the lady's house and, while she instructed us in just how to do it without damaging the instrument or ourselves, we moved it, by slow degrees, from the dining room to the parlor.

Now read those pamphlets, Miss Balaifal said.

Yes, ma'am, Pandro said. Is that all?

Well, now, the lady said. I want you to sing while I play the organ.

I can't sing, Miss Balaifum, Pandro said.

Nonsense, the lady said. Of course you can sing, Pedro.

Pandro, not Pedro, Pandro said. Pedro is my cousin's name.

As a matter of fact Pandro's name was Pantalo, which in Armenian means pants. When he had started to school his teacher hadn't cared for, or hadn't liked the sound of, the name, so she had written down on his card Pandro. As for his cousin's name, it was Bedros, with the *b* soft, which in turn had been changed at school to Pedro. It was all quite all right of course, and no harm to anybody.

Without answering him, the elderly lady sat on the stool, adjusted her feet on the pedals of the organ, and without any instructions to us, began to play a song which, from its dullness, was obviously religious. After a moment she herself began to sing. Pandro, in a soft voice, uttered a very profane, if not vulgar, word, which fortunately Miss Balaifal did not hear. Miss Balaifal's voice was, if anything, not impressive. The pedals squeaked a good deal louder than she sang, the tones of the organ were not any too clear, but even so, it was possible to know that Miss Balaifal's voice was not delightful.

Galilee, bright Galilee, she sang.

She turned to us, nodded, and said, Now sing. Sing, boys.

We knew neither the words nor the music, but it seemed that common courtesy demanded at least an honest effort, which we made, trying as far as possible to follow the music coming out of the organ and the dramatic words coming out of Miss Balaifal.

Ruler of the storm was He, on the raging Galilee, she sang.

In all, we tried to sing three songs. After each song, Pandro would say, Thank you very much, Miss Balaifum. Can we go now?

At last she got up from the organ and said, I'm

sure you're the better for it. If evil friends invite you to drink, turn away.

We'll turn away, Miss Balaifum, Pandro said. Won't we, Aram?

I will, I said.

I will too, Pandro said. Can we go now, Miss Balaifum?

Read the pamphlets, she said. It's not too late.

We'll read them, Pandro said. Just as soon as we get time.

We left the lady's house and went back to the front yard of Pandro's house and began to read the pamphlets. Before we were half through reading, the lady came out on the porch and in a very high and excited voice said, Which of you was it?

Which of us was *what?* Pandro said.

He was very bewildered.

Which of you was it that *sang?* Miss Balaifal said.

We both sang, I said.

No, Miss Balaifal said. Only one of you sang. One of you has a beautiful Christian voice.

Not me, Pandro said.

You, Miss Balaifal said to me. Eugene. Was it you?

Aram, I said. Not Eugene. No, I don't think it was me either.

Boys, come here, Miss Balaifal said.

Who? Pandro said.

Both of you, the lady said.

When we were in the house and Miss Balaifal was seated at the organ again Pandro said, I don't want to sing. I don't like to sing.

You sing, the lady said to me.

I sang.

Miss Balaifal leaped to her feet.

You are the one, she said. You must sing at church.

I won't, I said.

You mustn't use profane language, she said.

I'm not using profane language, I said, and I promise not to use profane language again as long as I live, but I won't sing in church.

Your voice is the most Christian voice I have ever heard, Miss Balaifal said.

It isn't, I said.

Yes, it is, she said.

Well, I won't sing anyway, I said.

You must, you must, Miss Balaifal said.

Thanks very much, Miss Balaifum, Pandro

said. Can we go now? He doesn't want to sing in church.

He must, he must, the lady insisted.

Why? Pandro said.

For the good of his soul, the lady said.

Pandro whispered the profane word again.

Now tell me, the lady said. What is your name?

I told her.

You are a Christian of course? she said.

I guess so, I said.

A Presbyterian of course, she said.

I don't know about that, I said.

You are, the lady said. Of course you are. I want you to sing in the Tulare Street Presbyterian Church—in the Boys' Choir—next Sunday.

Why? Pandro said again.

We need voices, the lady explained. We must have young voices. We must have singers. He must sing next Sunday.

I don't like to sing, I said. I don't like to go to church either.

Boys, Miss Balaifal said. Sit down. I want to talk to you.

We sat down. Miss Balaifal talked to us for at least thirty minutes.

We didn't believe a word of it, although out of

courtesy we kept answering her questions the way we knew she wanted us to answer them, but when she asked us to get down on our knees with her while she prayed, we wouldn't do it. Miss Balaifal argued this point for some time and then decided to let us have our way—for a moment. Then she tried again, but we wouldn't do it. Pandro said we'd move the organ any time, or anything else like that, but we wouldn't get down on our knees.

Well, Miss Balaifal said, will you close your eyes?

What for? Pandro said.

It's customary for everybody to close his eyes while someone is praying, Miss Balaifal said.

Who's praying? Pandro said.

No one, *yet,* Miss Balaifal said. But if you'll promise to close your eyes, *I'll* pray, but you've got to promise to close your eyes.

What do you want to pray for? Pandro said.

I want to pray for you boys, she said.

What for? Pandro said.

A little prayer for you won't do any harm, Miss Balaifal said. Will you close your eyes?

Oh! all right, Pandro said.

We closed our eyes and Miss Balaifal prayed.

It wasn't a little prayer by a long shot.

Amen, she said. Now, boys, don't you feel better?

In all truth, we didn't.

Yes, we do, Pandro said. Can we go now, Miss Balaifum? Any time you want the organ moved, we'll move it for you.

Sing for all you're worth, Miss Balaifal said to me, and turn away from any evil companion who invites you to drink.

Yes, ma'am, I said.

You know where the church is, she said.

What church? I said.

The Tulare Street Presbyterian Church, she said.

I know where it is, I said.

Mr. Sherwin will be expecting you Sunday morning at nine-thirty, she said.

Well, it just seemed like I was cornered.

Pandro went with me to the church on Sunday, but refused to stand with the choir boys and sing. He sat in the last row of the church and watched and listened. As for myself, I was never more unhappy in my life, although I sang.

Never again, I told Pandro after it was all over.

The following Sunday I didn't show up of course, but that didn't do any good, because Miss

Balaifal got us into her house again, played the organ, sang, made us try to sing, prayed, and was unmistakably determined to keep me in the Boys' Choir. I refused flatly, and Miss Balaifal decided to put the whole thing on a more worldly basis.

You have a rare Christian voice, she explained. A voice needed by religion. You yourself are deeply religious, although you do not know it yet. Since this is so, let me ask you to sing for *me* every Sunday. I will *pay* you.

How much? Pandro said.

Fifty cents, Miss Balaifal said.

We usually sang four or five songs. It took about half an hour altogether, although we had to sit another hour while the preacher delivered his sermon. In short, it wasn't worth it.

For this reason I could make no reply.

Seventy-five cents, Miss Balaifal suggested.

The air was stuffy, the preacher was a bore, it was all very depressing.

One dollar, Miss Balaifal said. Not a cent more.

Make it a dollar and a quarter, Pandro said.

Not a cent more than a dollar, Miss Balaifal said.

He's got the best voice in the whole choir,

Pandro said. *One* dollar? A voice like that is worth *two* dollars to any religion.

I've made my offer, Miss Balaifal said.

There are other religions, Pandro said.

This, I must say, upset Miss Balaifal.

His voice, she said bitterly, is a Christian voice, and what's more it's Presbyterian.

The Baptists would be glad to get a voice like that for two dollars, Pandro said.

The Baptists! Miss Balaifal said with some—I hesitate to say it—contempt.

They're no different than the Presbyterams, Pandro said.

One dollar, Miss Balaifal said. One dollar, and your name on the program.

I don't like to sing, Miss Balaifal, I said.

Yes, you do, she said. You just think you don't. If you could see your face when you sing—why—

He's got a voice like an angel, Pandro said.

I'll fix you, I told Pandro in Armenian.

That's no one-dollar voice, Pandro said.

All right, boys, Miss Balaifal said. A dollar and fifteen cents, but no more.

A dollar and a quarter, Pandro said, or we go to the Baptists.

All right, Miss Balaifal said, but I must say you drive a hard bargain.

Wait a minute, I said. I don't like to sing. I won't sing for a dollar and a quarter or anything else.

A bargain is a bargain, Miss Balaifal said.

I didn't make any bargain, I said. Pandro did. Let *him* sing.

He *can't* sing, Miss Balaifal said.

I've got the worst voice in the world, Pandro said with great pride.

His poor voice wouldn't be worth ten cents to anybody, Miss Balaifal said.

Not even a nickel, Pandro said.

Well, I said, I'm not going to sing—for a dollar and a quarter or anything else. I don't need any money.

You made a bargain, Miss Balaifal said.

Yes, you did, Pandro said.

I jumped on Pandro right in Miss Balaifal's parlor and we began to wrestle. The elderly Christian lady tried to break it up, but since it was impossible to determine which of us was the boy with the angelic voice, she began to pray. The wrestling continued until most of the furniture in the room had been knocked over, except the

126

organ. The match was eventually a draw, the wrestlers exhausted and flat on their backs.

Miss Balaifal stopped praying and said, Sunday then, at a dollar and a quarter.

It took me some time to get my breath.

Miss Balaifal, I said, I'll sing in that choir only if Pandro sings too.

But his voice, Miss Balaifal objected. It's horrible.

I don't care what it is, I said. If I sing, he's got to sing too.

I'm afraid he'd ruin the choir, Miss Balaifal said.

He's got to go up there with me every Sunday, I said, or nothing doing.

Well, now, let me see, Miss Balaifal said.

She gave the matter considerable thought.

Suppose he goes up and stands in the choir, Miss Balaifal said, but *doesn't* sing? Suppose he just *pretends* to sing?

That's all right with me, I said, but he's got to be there all the time.

What do *I* get? Pandro said.

Well, now, Miss Balaifal said, I surely can't be expected to pay you, too.

127

If I go up there, Pandro said, I've got to be paid.

All right, Miss Balaifal said. One dollar for the boy who sings; twenty-five cents for the boy who doesn't.

I've got the worst voice in the world, Pandro said.

You must be fair, Miss Balaifal said. After all, you won't be singing. You'll just be standing there with the other boys.

Twenty-five cents isn't enough, Pandro said.

We got off the floor and began rearranging the furniture.

All right, Miss Balaifal said. One dollar for the boy who sings. Thirty-five cents for the boy who doesn't.

Make it fifty, Pandro said.

Very well, then, Miss Balaifal said. A dollar for *you*. Fifty cents for *you*.

We start working next Sunday? Pandro said.

That's right, Miss Balaifal said. I'll pay you here after the services. Not a word of this to any of the other boys in the choir.

We won't mention it to anybody, Pandro said.

In this manner, in the eleventh year of my life, I became, more or less, a Presbyterian—at least every Sunday morning. It wasn't the money. It was simply that a bargain had been made, and that Miss Balaifal had her heart set on having me sing for religion.

As I began to say six or seven minutes ago, however, a curious thing about our country is the ease with which all of us—or at least everybody I know—are able to change our religions, without any noticeable damage to anything or anybody. When I was thirteen I was baptized into the Armenian Catholic Church, even though I was still singing for the Presbyterians, and even though I myself was growing a little skeptical, as it were, of the whole conventional religious pattern, and was eager, by hook or crook, to reach an understanding of my own, and to come to terms with Omnipotence in my own way. Even after I was baptized, I carried in my heart a deep discontent.

Two months after I was baptized my voice changed, and my contract with Miss Balaifal was canceled—which was a great relief to me and a terrible blow to her.

As for the Armenian Catholic Church on Ventura Avenue, I went there only on Easter and Christmas. All the rest of the time I moved from

one religion to another, and in the end was none
the worse for it, so that now, like most Americans,
my faith consists in believing in every religion,
including my own, but without any ill-will toward
anybody, no matter what he believes or disbe-
lieves, just so his personality is good.

THE CIRCUS

ANY time a circus used to come to town, that was all me and my old pal Joey Renna needed to make us run hog-wild, as the saying is. All we needed to do was see the signs on the fences and in the empty store windows to start going to the dogs and neglecting our educations. All we needed to know was that a circus was on its way to town for me and Joey to start wanting to know what good a little education ever did anybody anyway.

After the circus *reached* town we were just no good at all. We spent all our time down at the trains, watching them unload the animals, walking out Ventura Avenue with the wagons with lions and tigers in them and hanging around the grounds, trying to win the favor of the animal men, the workers, the acrobats, and the clowns.

The circus was everything everything else we

knew wasn't. It was adventure, travel, danger, skill, grace, romance, comedy, peanuts, popcorn, chewing-gum and soda-water. We used to carry water to the elephants and stand around afterwards and try to seem associated with the whole magnificent affair, the putting up of the big tent, the getting everything in order, and the worldly-wise waiting for the people to come and spend their money.

One day Joey came tearing into the classroom of the fifth grade at Emerson School ten minutes late, and without so much as removing his hat or trying to explain his being late, shouted, Hey, Aram, what the hell are you doing here? The circus is in town.

And sure enough I'd forgotten. I jumped up and ran out of the room with poor old Miss Flibety screaming after me, Aram Garoghlanian, you stay in this room. Do you hear me, Aram Garoghlanian?

I heard her all right and I knew what my not staying would mean. It would mean another powerful strapping from old man Dawson. But I couldn't help it. I was just crazy about a circus.

I been looking all over for you, Joey said in the street. What happened?

I forgot, I said. I knew it was coming all right, but I forgot it was today. How far along are they?

I was at the trains at five, Joey said. I been out at the grounds since seven. I had breakfast at the circus table. Boy, it was good.

Honest, Joey? I said. How were they?

They're all swell, Joey said. Couple more years, they told me, and I'll be ready to go away with them.

As what? I said. Lion-tamer, or something like that?

I guess maybe not as a lion-tamer, Joey said. I figure more like a workman till I learn about being a clown or something, I guess. I don't figure I could work with lions right away.

We were out on Ventura Avenue, headed for the circus grounds, out near the County Fairgrounds, just north of the County Hospital.

Boy, what a breakfast, Joey said. Hot-cakes, ham and eggs, sausages, coffee. Boy.

Why didn't you tell me? I said.

I thought you knew, Joey said. I thought you'd be down at the trains same as last year. I would have told you if I knew you'd forgotten. What made you forget?

I don't know, I said. Nothing, I guess.

I was wrong there, but I didn't know it at the time. I hadn't really forgotten. What I'd done was *remembered*. I'd gone to work and remembered the strapping Dawson gave me last year for staying out of school the day the circus was in town. That was the thing that had kind of kept me sleeping after four-thirty in the morning when by rights I should have been up and dressing and on my way to the trains. It was the memory of that strapping old man Dawson had given me, but I didn't know it at the time. We used to take them strappings kind of for granted, me and Joey, on account of we wanted to be fair and square with the Board of Education and if it was against the rules to stay out of school when you weren't sick, and if you were supposed to get strapped for doing it, well, there we were, we'd done it, so let the Board of Education balance things the best way they knew how. They did that with a strapping. They used to threaten to send me and Joey to Reform School but they never did it.

Circus? old man Dawson used to say. I see. *Circus.* Well, bend down, boy.

So, first Joey, then me, would bend down and old man Dawson would get some powerful shoulder exercise while we tried not to howl. We

wouldn't howl for five or six licks, but after that
we'd howl like Indians coming. They used to be
able to hear us all over the school and old man
Dawson, after our visits got to be kind of regular,
urged us politely to try to make a little less noise,
inasmuch as it was a school and people were trying to study.

It ain't fair to the others, old man Dawson said.
They're trying to learn something for themselves.

We can't help it, Joey said. It hurts.

That I know, old man Dawson said, but it
seems to me there's such a thing as modulation. I
believe a lad can overdo his howling if he ain't
thoughtful of others. Just try to modulate that
awful howl a little. I think you can do it.

Then he gave Joey a strapping of twenty and
Joey tried his best not to howl so loud. After the
strapping his face was very red and old man Dawson was very tired.

How was that? Joey said.

That was better, old man Dawson said. By far
the most courteous you've managed yet.

I did my best, Joey said.

I'm grateful to you, old man Dawson said.

He was tired and out of breath. I moved up to
the chair in front of him that he furnished during

these matters to help us suffer the stinging pain. I got in the right position and he said, Wait a minute, Aram. Give a man a chance to get his breath. I'm not twenty-three years old. I'm *sixty*-three. Let me rest a minute.

All right, I said, but I sure would like to get this over with.

Don't howl too loud, he said. Folks passing by in the street are liable to think this is a veritable chamber of tortures. Does it really hurt that much?

You can ask Joey, I said.

How about it, Joey? old man Dawson said. Aren't you lads exaggerating just a little? Perhaps to impress someone in your room? Some girl, perhaps?

We don't howl to impress anybody, Mr. Dawson, Joey said. We wouldn't howl if we could help it. Howling makes us feel ashamed, doesn't it, Aram?

It's awfully embarrassing to go back to our seats in our room after howling that way, I said. We'd rather not howl if we could help it.

Well, old man Dawson said, I'll not be unreasonable. I'll only ask you to try to modulate it a little.

I'll do my best, Mr. Dawson, I said. Got your breath back?

Give me just a moment longer, Aram, Mr. Dawson said.

When he got his breath back he gave me my twenty and I howled a little louder than Joey and then we went back to class. It was awfully embarrassing. Everybody was looking at us.

Well, Joey said, what did you expect? The rest of you would fall down and die if you got twenty. You wouldn't *howl a little*, you'd die.

That'll be enough out of you, Miss Flibety said.

Well, it's true, Joey said. They're all scared. A circus comes to town and what do they do? They come to school. They don't go out to the circus.

That'll be enough, Miss Flibety said.

Who do they think they are, giving us dirty looks? Joey said.

Miss Flibety lifted her hand, hushing Joey.

Now the circus was back in town, another year had gone by, it was April again, and we were on our way out to the grounds. Only this time it was worse than ever because they'd seen us at school and knew we were going out to the circus.

Do you think they'll send Stafford after us? I said.

Stafford was truant officer.

We can always run, Joey said. If he comes, I'll go one way, you go another. He can't chase *both* of us. At least one of us will get away.

All right, I said. Suppose one of us gets caught?

Well, let's see, Joey said. Should the one who isn't caught give himself up or should he wreck Stafford's Ford?

I vote for wreck, I said.

So do I, Joey said, so wreck it is.

When we got out to the grounds a couple of the little tents were up, and the big one was going up. We stood around and watched. It was great the way they did it. Just a handful of guys who looked like tramps doing work you'd think no less than a hundred men could do. Doing it with style, too.

All of a sudden a man everybody called Red hollered at me and Joey.

Here, you Arabs, he said, give us a hand.

Me and Joey ran over to him.

Yes, sir, I said.

He was a small man with very broad shoulders and very big hands. You didn't feel that he was small, because he seemed so powerful and because he had so much thick red hair on his head. You thought he was practically a giant.

He handed me and Joey a rope. The rope was attached to some canvas that was lying on the ground.

This is going to be easy, Red said. As the boys lift the pole and get it in place you keep pulling the rope, so the canvas will go up with the pole.

Yes, sir, Joey said.

Everybody was busy when we saw Stafford.

We can't run now, I said.

Let him come, Joey said. We told Red we'd give him a hand and we're going to do it.

I'll tell you what, I said. We'll tell him we'll go with him after we get the canvas up; then we'll run.

All right, Joey said.

Stafford was a big fellow in a business suit who had a beef-red face and looked as if he ought to be a lawyer or something. He came over and said, All right, you hooligans, come along with me.

We promised to give Red a hand, Joey said. We'll come just as soon as we get this canvas up.

We were pulling for all we were worth, slipping and falling. The men were all working hard. Red was hollering orders, and then the whole thing was over and we had done our part.

We didn't even get a chance to find out what

Red was going to say to us, or if he was going to invite us to sit at the table for lunch, or what.

Joey busted loose and ran one way and I ran the other and Stafford came after *me*. I heard the circus men laughing and Red hollering, Run, boy, run. He can't catch *you*. He's soft. Give him a good run. He needs the exercise.

I could hear Stafford, too. He was very sore and he was cussing.

I got away, though, and stayed low until I saw him drive off in his Ford. Then I went back to the big tent and found Joey.

We'll get it this time, Joey said.

I guess it'll be Reform School this time, I said.

No, Joey said. I guess it'll be thirty. We're going to do some awful howling if it is. Thirty's a lot of whacks even if he *is* sixty-three years old. He ain't exactly a weakling.

Thirty? I said. Ouch. That's liable to make me cry.

Maybe, Joey said. Me too, maybe. Seems like ten can make you cry, then you hold off till it's eleven, then twelve, and you think you'll start crying on the next one, but you don't. We haven't so far, anyway. Maybe we will when it's thirty.

Oh, well, I said, that's tomorrow.

Red gave us some more work to do around the grounds and let us sit next to him at lunch. It was swell. We talked to some acrobats who were Spanish, and to a family of Italians who worked with horses. We saw both shows, the afternoon one and the evening one, and then we helped with the work, taking the circus to pieces again; then we went down to the trains, and then home. I got home real late. In the morning I was sleepy when I had to get up for school.

They were waiting for us. Miss Flibety didn't even let us sit down for the roll call. She just told us to go to the office. Old man Dawson was waiting for us, too. Stafford was there, too, and very sore.

I figured, Well, here's where we go to Reform School.

Here they are, Mr. Dawson said to Stafford. Take them away, if you like.

It was easy to tell they'd been talking for some time and hadn't been getting along any too well. Old man Dawson seemed irritated and Stafford seemed sore at him.

In *this* school, old man Dawson said, I do any punishing that's got to be done. Nobody else. I can't stop you from taking them to Reform School, though.

Stafford didn't say anything. He just left the office.

Well, lads, old man Dawson said. How was it?

We had lunch with them, Joey said.

Let's see now, old man Dawson said. What offense is this, the sixteenth or the seventeenth?

It ain't that many, Joey said. Must be eleven or twelve.

Well, old man Dawson said, I'm sure of one thing. This is the time I'm supposed to make it thirty.

I think the next one is the one you're supposed to make thirty, Joey said.

No, Mr. Dawson said, we've lost track somewhere, but I'm sure this is the time it goes up to thirty. Who's going to be first?

Me, I said.

All right, Aram, Mr. Dawson said. Take a good hold on the chair, brace yourself, and try to modulate your howl.

Yes, sir, I said. I'll do my best, but thirty's an awful lot.

Well, a funny thing happened. He gave me thirty all right and I howled all right, but it *was* a modulated howl. It was the most modulated howl I ever howled; because it was the *easiest* strapping I ever got. I counted them and there were thirty all right, but they didn't hurt, so I didn't cry, as I was afraid I might.

It was the same with Joey. We stood together waiting to be dismissed.

I'm awfully grateful to you boys, old man Dawson said, for modulating your howls so nicely this time. I don't want people to think I'm killing you.

We wanted to thank him for giving us such easy strappings, but we couldn't say it. I think he knew the way we felt, though, because he smiled in a way that gave us an idea he knew.

Then we went back to class.

It was swell because we knew everything would be all right till the County Fair opened in September.

THE THREE SWIMMERS

AND THE GROCER FROM

YALE

THE ditches were dry most of the year, but when they weren't dry, they were roaring. As the snows melted in the hills the ditches began to roar and from somewhere, God knows where, arrived frogs and turtles, water snakes and fish. In the spring of the year the water hurried, and with it the heart, but as the fields changed from green to brown, the blossoms to fruit, the shy warmth to arrogant heat, the ditches slowed down and the heart grew lazy. The first water from the hills was cold, swift, and frightening. It was too cold and busy to invite the naked body of a boy.

Alone, or in a group, a boy would stand on the bank of a ditch and watch the water for many minutes, and then, terribly challenged, fling off his clothes, make a running dive, come up gasping, and swim across to the other side. If the boy was the first of a group to dive, the others would

soon follow, in order not to walk home in shame.
It wasn't simply that the water was cold. It was
more that it had no time for boys. The springtime
water was as unfriendly as anything could be.

One day in April I set out for Thompson Ditch
with my cousin Mourad and a pal of his named
Joe Bettencourt, a Portuguese who loved nothing
more than to be free and out-of-doors. A school-
room made Joe stupid. It embarrassed him. But
once out of school, once off the school-grounds, he
was as intelligent, as good-natured, casual, sin-
cere, and friendly as anyone could possibly be. As
my cousin Mourad said, Joe ain't dumb—he just
doesn't want an education.

It was a bright Saturday morning. We had two
baloney sandwiches each, and ten cents between
the three of us. We decided to walk to the ditch
so that we would get there around noon, when
the day would be warm. We walked along the rail-
road tracks to Calwa. Along the state highway to
Malaga. And then east through the vineyard country to the ditch. When we said Thompson Ditch,
we meant a specific place. It was an intersection
of country roads, with a wooden bridge and a
headgate. The swimming was south of the bridge.
West of the ditch was a big fenced-in pasture, with

cows and horses grazing in it. East of the ditch was
the country road. The road and the ditch traveled
together many miles. The flow was south, and the
next bridge was two miles away. In the summertime a day of swimming was incomplete until a
boy had gone downstream to the other bridge,
rested a moment in the pasture land, and then
came back up, against the stream, which was a
good workout.

By the time we got out to Thompson Ditch the
brightness of morning had changed to a gloom
that was unmistakably wintry; in fact, the beginning of a storm. The water was roaring, the sky
was gray, growing black, the air was cold and unfriendly, and the landscape seemed lonely and des-
olate.

Joe Bettencourt said, I came all this way to
swim and rain or no rain I'm going to swim.

So am I, I said.

You wait, my cousin Mourad said. Me and Joe
will see how it is. If it's all right, you can come in.
Can you really swim?

Aw shut up, I said.

This is what I always said when it seemed to me
that somebody had unwittingly insulted me.

Well, Joe said, *can* you?

Sure I can swim, I said.

If you ask *him,* my cousin Mourad said, he can do anything. Better than anybody in the world.

Neither of them knew how uncertain I was as to whether or not I could swim well enough to negotiate a dive and a swim across that body of cold roaring water. If the truth were known, when I saw the dark water roaring I was scared, challenged, and insulted.

Aw shut up, I said to the water.

I brought out my lunch and bit into one of the sandwiches. My cousin Mourad whacked my hand and almost knocked the sandwich into the water.

We eat after we swim, he said. Do you want to have cramps?

I had plumb forgotten. It was because I was so challenged and scared.

One sandwich won't give anybody cramps, I said.

It'll taste better after we swim, Joe said.

He was a very kind boy. He knew I was scared and he knew I was bluffing. I knew *he* was scared, but I knew he was figuring everything out a little more wisely than I was.

Let's see, he said. We'll swim across, rest, swim back, get dressed, eat, and unless the storm passes,

start for home. Otherwise we'll swim some more.
This storm isn't going to pass, my cousin
Mourad said. If we're going to swim, we're going
to have to do it in a hurry and start for home.

By this time Joe was taking off his clothes. My
cousin Mourad was taking off his, and I was taking off mine. We stood together naked on the
bank of the ditch looking at the unfriendly water.
It certainly didn't invite a dive, but there was no
other honorable way to enter a body of water. If
you tried to walk in, you were just naturally not
a swimmer. If you jumped in feet first it wasn't exactly a disgrace, it was just bad style. On the other
hand, the water was utterly without charm, altogether unfriendly, uninviting, and sinister. It was
certainly challenging, though. The swiftness of
the water made the distance to the opposite bank
seem greater than it was.

Without a word Joe dived in. Without a word
my cousin Mourad dived in. The second or two
between splashes seemed like long days dreamed
in a winter dream because I was not only scared
but very cold. With a bookful of unspoken words
on my troubled mind, I dived in.

The next thing I knew—and it wasn't more
than three seconds later—I was listening to Joe

yelling, my cousin Mourad yelling, and myself yelling. What had happened was that we had all dived into mud up to our elbows, had gotten free only with great effort, and had each come up worrying about what had happened to the other two. We were all standing in the cold roaring water, up to our knees in soft mud.

The dives had been standing dives. If they had been running dives we would have stuck in the mud up to our ankles, head first, and remained there until summer, or later.

This scared us a little on the one hand and on the other hand made us feel very lucky to be alive.

The storm broke while we stood in the mud of the ditch.

Well, Joe said, we're going to get caught in the rain anyhow. We might as well stay in a little while anyway.

We were all shivering, but it seemed sensible that we should try our best to make a swim of it. The water wasn't three feet deep; nevertheless, Joe managed to leap out of the mud and swim across, and then back.

We swam for what seemed like a long time, but was probably no more than ten minutes. Then we got out of the water and mud and dressed and, standing under a tree, ate our sandwiches.

Instead of stopping, the rain increased, so we decided to set out for home right away.

We may get a ride, Joe said.

All the way to Malaga the country road was deserted. In Malaga we went into the general store and warmed ourselves at the stove and chipped in and bought a can of beans and a loaf of French bread. The proprietor of the store was a man named Darcous who wasn't a foreigner. He opened the can for us, divided the beans into three parts on three paper plates, gave us each a wooden fork, and sliced the bread for us. He was an old man who seemed funny and young.

Where you been, boys? he said.

Swimming, Joe said.

Swimming? he said.

Sure, Joe said. We showed that river.

Well, I'll be harrowed, the grocer said. How was it?

Not three feet deep, Joe said.

Cold?

Ice-cold.

Well, I'll be cultivated, the grocer said. Did you have fun?

Did we? Joe asked my cousin Mourad.

Joe didn't know whether it had been fun or something else.

I don't know, my cousin Mourad said. When we dived in we got stuck in the mud up to our elbows.

It wasn't easy to get loose from the mud, I said.

Well, I'll be pruned, the grocer said.

He opened a second can of beans, pitched an enormous forkful into his mouth, and then divided the rest onto the three paper plates.

We haven't got any more money, I said.

Now, tell me, boys, the grocer said, what made you do it?

Nothing, Joe said with the finality of a boy who has too many reasons to enumerate at a moment's notice, and his mouth full of beans and French bread.

Well, I'll be gathered into a pile and burned, the grocer said. Now, boys, he said, tell me—of what race are you? Californians, or foreigners?

We're all Californians, Joe said. I was born on G Street in Fresno. Mourad here was born on Walnut Avenue or someplace on the other side of the Southern Pacific tracks, I guess, and his cousin somewhere around in that neighborhood, too.

Well, I'll be irrigated, the grocer said. Now, tell me, boys, what sort of educations have you got?

We ain't educated, Joe said.

Well, I'll be picked off a tree and thrown into a box, the grocer said. Now, tell me, boys, what foreign languages do you speak?

I speak Portuguese, Joe said.

You ain't educated? the grocer said. I have a degree from Yale, my boy, and I can't speak Portuguese. And you, son, how about you?

I speak Armenian, my cousin Mourad said.

Well, I'll be cut off a vine and eaten grape by grape by a girl in her teens, the grocer said. I can't speak a word of Armenian and I'm a college graduate, class of 1892. Now, tell me, son, he said. What's *your* name?

Aram Garoghlanian, I said.

I think I can get it, he said. Gar-oghlan-ian. Is that it?

That's it, I said.

Aram, he said.

Yes, sir, I said.

And what strange foreign language do *you* speak? he said.

I speak Armenian, too, I said. That's my cousin. *Mourad* Garoghlanian.

Well, I'll be harrowed, he said, cultivated, pruned, gathered into a pile, burned, picked off a tree, and let me see what else? Thrown into a box, I think it was, cut off a vine and eaten grape by grape by a girl in her teens. Yes, sir. All them things, if this doesn't beat everything. Did you encounter any reptiles?

What's reptiles? Joe said.

Snakes, the grocer said.

We didn't see any, Joe said. The water was black.

Black water, the grocer said. Any fish?

Didn't see any, Joe said.

A Ford stopped in front of the store and an old man got out and came across the wood floor of the porch into the store.

Open me a bottle, Abbott, the man said.

Judge Harmon, the grocer said, I want you to meet three of the most heroic Californians of this great state.

The grocer pointed at Joe, and Joe said, Joseph Bettencourt—I speak Portuguese.

Stephen L. Harmon, the Judge said. I speak a
little French.

The grocer pointed at my cousin Mourad and
Mourad said, Mourad Garoghlanian.

What do you speak? the Judge said.

Armenian, my cousin Mourad said.

The grocer gave the Judge the opened bottle,
the Judge lifted it to his lips, swallowed three
swigs, beat his chest, and said, I'm mighty proud
to meet a Californian who speaks Armenian.

The grocer pointed at me.

Aram Garoghlanian, I said.

Brothers? the Judge asked.

Cousins, I said.

Same thing, the Judge said. Now, Abbott, if you
please, what's the occasion for this banquet and
your poetic excitement, if not delirium?

The boys have just come from showing that old
river, the grocer said.

The Judge took three more swigs, beat his chest
three times slowly and said, Come from *what?*

They've just come from swimming, the grocer
said.

Have any of you fevers? the Judge said.

Fever? Joe said. We ain't sick.

The grocer busted out with a roar of laughter.

Sick? he said. Sick? Judge, these boys dived naked into the black water of winter and came up glowing with the warmth of summer.

We finished the beans and the bread. We were thirsty but didn't know if we should intrude with a request for a drink of water. At least *I* didn't know, but Joe apparently didn't stop to consider.

Mr. Abbott, he said, could we have a drink of water?

Water? the grocer said. Water, my boy? Water's for swimming in, not for drinking.

He fetched three paper cups, went to a small barrel with a tap, turned the tap, and filled each cup with a light golden fluid.

Here, boys, he said. Drink. Drink the lovely juice of the golden apple, unfermented.

The Judge poured the grocer a drink out of his bottle, lifted the bottle to his lips, and said, To your health, gentlemen.

Yes, sir, Joe said.

We all drank.

The Judge screwed the top onto the bottle, put the bottle into his back pocket, looked at each of us carefully, as if to remember us for the rest of his life, and said, Good-by, gentlemen. Court opens in a half hour. I must pass sentence on a man who says he *borrowed* the horse, *didn't* steal it. He speaks Mexican. The man who says he *stole* the horse speaks Italian. Good-by.

Good-by, we said.

By this time our clothes were almost dry, but the rain hadn't stopped.

Well, Joe said, thanks very much, Mr. Abbott. We've got to get home.

Not at all, the grocer said. *I* thank you.

The grocer seemed to be in a strange silence for a man who only a moment before had been so noisy with talk.

We left the store quietly and began to walk down the highway. The rain was now so light it didn't seem like rain at all. I didn't know what to make of it. Joe was the first to speak.

That Mr. Abbott, he said, he's some man.

The name on the sign is Darcous, I said. Abbott's his first name.

First or last, Joe said, he sure is some man.

That Judge was somebody too, my cousin Mourad said.

Educated, Joe said. I'd learn French myself, but who would I talk to?

We walked along the highway in silence. After a few minutes the black clouds parted, the sun came through, and away over in the east we saw the rainbow over the Sierra Nevadas.

We sure showed that old river, Joe said. Was he crazy?

I don't know, my cousin Mourad said.

It took us another hour to get home. We had all thought about the two men and whether or not the grocer was crazy. Myself, I believed he wasn't, but at the same time it seemed to me he had acted kind of crazy.

So long, Joe said.

So long, we said.

He went down the street. Fifty yards away he turned around and said something almost to himself.

What? my cousin Mourad shouted.

He was, Joe said.

Was what? I shouted.

Crazy, Joe shouted back.

Yeah? I shouted back. How do you know?

How can you be cut off a vine and eaten grape by grape by a girl in her teens? Joe shouted.

Suppose he was crazy? my cousin Mourad said. What of it?

Joe put his hand to his chin and began to consider. The sun was shining for all it was worth now and the world was full of light.

I don't think he was crazy, he shouted.

He went on down the street.

He was pretty crazy, my cousin Mourad said.

Well, I said, maybe he's not always.

We decided to let the matter rest at this point until we went swimming again, at which time we would visit the store again and see what happened.

A month later when, after swimming in the ditch, the three of us went into the store, the man who was in charge was a much younger man than Mr. Abbott Darcous. He wasn't a foreigner either.

What'll it be? he said.

A nickel's worth of baloney, Joe said, and a loaf of French bread.

Where's Mr. Darcous? my cousin Mourad said.

He's gone home, the young man said.

Where's that? I said.

Some place in Connecticut, I think, the young man said.

We made sandwiches of the baloney and French bread and began to eat.

At last Joe asked the question.

Was he crazy? Joe said.

Well, the young man said, that's hard to say. I thought he was crazy at first. Then I decided he wasn't. The way he ran this store made you think he was crazy. He gave away more than he sold. To hear him talk you'd think he was crazy. Otherwise he was all right.

Thanks, Joe said.

The store was all in order now, and a very dull place. We walked out, and began walking home.

He's crazy, Joe said.

Who? I said.

That guy in the store now, Joe said.

That young fellow? I said.

Yeah, Joe said. That new fellow in there that ain't got no education.

I think you're right, my cousin Mourad said.

All the way home we remembered the educated grocer.

Well, I'll be cultivated, Joe said when he left us and walked on down the street.

Well, I'll be picked off a tree and thrown in a box, my cousin Mourad said.

Well, I'll be cut off a vine and eaten grape by grape by a girl in her teens, I said.

The Three Swimmers

He sure was some man. Twenty years later, I decided he had been a poet and had run that grocery store in that little run-down village just for the casual poetry in it instead of the paltry cash.

LOCOMOTIVE 38, THE

OJIBWAY

ONE day a man came to town on a donkey and began loafing around in the public library where I used to spend most of my time in those days. He was a tall young Indian of the Ojibway tribe. He told me his name was Locomotive 38. Everybody in town believed he had escaped from an asylum.

Six days after he arrived in town his animal was struck by the Tulare Street trolley and seriously injured. The following day the animal passed away, most likely of internal injuries, on the corner of Mariposa and Fulton streets. The animal sank to the pavement, fell on the Indian's leg, groaned and died. When the Indian got his leg free he got up and limped into the drug store on the corner and made a long distance telephone call. He telephoned his brother in Oklahoma. The call cost him a lot of money, which he dropped into the slot as requested by the operator as if he were in the habit of making such calls every day.

I was in the drug store at the time, eating a Royal Banana Special, with crushed walnuts.

When he came out of the telephone booth he saw me sitting at the soda fountain eating this fancy dish.

Hello, Willie, he said.

He knew my name wasn't Willie—he just liked to call me that.

He limped to the front of the store where the gum was, and bought three packages of Juicy Fruit. Then he limped back to me and said, What's that you're eating, Willie? It looks good.

This is what they call a Royal Banana Special, I said.

The Indian got up on the stool next to me.

Give me the same, he said to the soda fountain girl.

That's too bad about your animal, I said.

There's no place for an animal in this world, he said. What kind of an automobile should I buy?

Are you going to buy an automobile? I said.

I've been thinking about it for several minutes now, he said.

I didn't think you had any money, I said. I
thought you were poor.

That's the impression people get, he said. Another impression they get is that I'm crazy.

I didn't get the impression that you were crazy,
I said, but I didn't get the impression that you
were rich, either.

Well, I am, the Indian said.

I wish I was rich, I said.

What for? he said.

Well, I said, I've been wanting to go fishing at
Mendota for three years in a row now. I need
some equipment and some kind of an automobile
to get out there in.

Can you drive an automobile? the Indian said.

I can drive anything, I said.

Have you ever driven an automobile? he said.

Not yet, I said. So far I haven't had any automobile to drive, and it's against my family religion
to steal an automobile.

Do you mean to tell me you believe you could
get into an automobile and start driving? he said.

That's right, I said.

Remember what I was telling you on the steps
of the public library the other evening? he said.

You mean about the machine age? I said.

Yes, he said.

I remember, I said.

All right, he said. Indians are born with an instinct for riding, rowing, hunting, fishing, and swimming. Americans are born with an instinct for fooling around with machines.

I'm no American, I said.

I know, the Indian said. You're an Armenian. I remember. I asked you and you told me. You're an Armenian born in America. You're fourteen years old and already you know you'll be able to drive an automobile the minute you get into one. You're a typical American, although your complexion, like my own, is dark.

Driving a car is no trick, I said. There's nothing to it. It's easier than riding a donkey.

All right, the Indian said. Just as you say. If I go up the street and buy an automobile, will you drive for me?

Of course, I said.

How much in wages would you want? he said.

You mean you want to give me wages for driving an automobile? I said.

Of course, the Ojibway said.

Well, I said, that's very nice of you, but I don't want any money for driving an automobile.

Some of the journeys may be long ones, he said.

The longer the better, I said.

Are you restless? he said.

I was born in this little old town, I said.

Don't you like it? he said.

I like mountains and streams and mountain lakes, I said.

Have you ever been in the mountains? he said.

Not yet, I said, but I'm going to reach them some day.

I see, he said. What kind of an automobile do you think I ought to buy?

How about a Ford roadster? I said.

Is that the best automobile? he said.

Do you want the *best*? I said.

Shouldn't I have the best? he said.

I don't know, I said. The best costs a lot of money.

What is the best? he said.

Well, I said, some people think the Cadillac is the best. Others like the Packard. They're both pretty good. I wouldn't know which is best. The Packard is beautiful to see going down the highway, but so is the Cadillac. I've watched a lot of them fine cars going down the highway.

How much is a Packard? he said.

Around three thousand dollars, I said. Maybe a little more.

Can we get one right away? he said.

I got down off the stool. He sounded crazy, but I knew he wasn't.

Listen, Mr. Locomotive, I said, do you really want to buy a Packard right away?

You know my animal passed away a few minutes ago, he said.

I saw it happen, I said. They'll probably be arresting you any minute now for leaving the animal in the street.

They won't arrest me, he said.

They will if there's a law against leaving a dead donkey in the street, I said.

No, they won't, he said.

Why not? I said.

Well, he said, they won't after I show them a few papers I carry around with me all the time. The people of this country have a lot of respect for money, and I've got a lot of money.

I guess he is crazy after all, I thought.

Where'd you get all this money? I said.

I own some land in Oklahoma, he said. About fifty thousand acres.

Is it worth money? I said.

No, he said. All but about twenty acres of it is worthless. I've got some oil wells on them twenty acres. My brother and I.

How did you Ojibways ever get down to Oklahoma? I said. I always thought the Ojibways lived up north, up around the Great Lakes.

That's right, the Indian said. We used to live up around the Great Lakes, but my grandfather was a pioneer. He moved west when everybody else did.

Oh, I said. Well, I guess they won't bother you about the dead donkey at that.

They won't bother me about anything, he said. It won't be because I've got money. It'll be because they think I'm crazy. Nobody in this town but you knows I've got money. Do you know where we can get one of them automobiles right away?

The Packard agency is up on Broadway, two blocks beyond the public library, I said.

All right, he said. If you're sure you won't mind driving for me, let's go get one of them. Something bright in color, he said. Red, if they've got red. Where would you like to drive to first?

Would you care to go fishing at Mendota? I said.

175

I'll take the ride, he said. I'll watch you fish. Where can we get some equipment for you?

Right around the corner at Homan's, I said.

We went around the corner to Homan's and the Indian bought twenty-seven dollars' worth of fishing equipment for me. Then we went up to the Packard agency on Broadway. They didn't have a red Packard, but there was a beautiful green one. It was light green, the color of new grass. This was back there in 1922. The car was a beautiful sports touring model.

Do you think you could drive this great big car? the Indian said.

I *know* I can drive it, I said.

The police found us in the Packard agency and wanted to arrest the Indian for leaving the dead donkey in the street. He showed them the papers he had told me about and the police apologized and went away. They said they'd removed the animal and were sorry they'd troubled him about it.

It's no trouble at all, he said.

He turned to the manager of the Packard agency, Jim Lewis, who used to run for Mayor every time election time came around.

I'll take this car, he said.

I'll draw up the papers immediately, Jim said.

What papers? the Indian said. I'm going to pay for it now.

You mean you want to pay three thousand two hundred seventeen dollars and sixty-five cents *cash?* Jim said.

Yes, the Indian said. It's ready to drive, isn't it?

Of course, Jim said. I'll have the boys go over it with a cloth to take off any dust on it. I'll have them check the motor too, and fill the gasoline tank. It won't take more than ten minutes. If you'll step into the office I'll close the transaction immediately.

Jim and the Indian stepped into Jim's office.

About three minutes later Jim came over to me, a man shaken to the roots.

Aram, he said, who is this guy? I thought he was a nut. I had Johnny telephone the Pacific-Southwest and they said his bank account is being transferred from somewhere in Oklahoma. They said his account is something over a million dollars. I thought he was a nut. Do you know him?

He told me his name is Locomotive 38, I said. That's no name.

That's a translation of his Indian name, Jim said. We've got his full name on the contract. Do you know him?

I've talked to him every day since he came to town on that donkey that died this morning, I said, but I never thought he had any money.

He says you're going to drive for him, Jim said. Are you sure you're the man to drive a great big car like this, son?

Wait a minute now, Mr. Lewis, I said. Don't try to push me out of this chance of a lifetime. I can drive this big Packard as well as anybody else in town.

I'm not trying to push you out of anything, Jim said. I just don't want you to drive out of here and run over six or seven innocent people and maybe smash the car. Get into the car and I'll give you a few pointers. Do you know anything about the gear shift?

I don't know anything about anything yet, I said, but I'll soon find out.

All right, Jim said. Just let me help you.

I got into the car and sat down behind the wheel. Jim got in beside me.

From now on, son, he said, I want you to regard me as a friend who will give you the shirt off his back. I want to thank you for bringing me this fine Indian gentleman.

He told me he wanted the best car on the mar-

ket, I said. You know I've always been crazy about
driving a Packard. Now how do I do it?

Well, Jim said, let's see.

He looked down at my feet.

My God, son, he said, your feet don't reach the
pedals.

Never mind that, I said. You just explain the
gear shift.

Jim explained everything while the boys wiped
the dust off the car and went over the motor and
filled the gasoline tank. When the Indian came
out and got into the car, in the back where I insisted he should sit, I had the motor going.

He says he knows how to drive, the Indian said
to Jim Lewis. By instinct, he said. I believe him,
too.

You needn't worry about Aram here, Jim said.
He can drive all right. Clear the way there, boys,
he shouted. Let him have all the room necessary.

I turned the big car around slowly, shifted, and
shot out of the agency at about fifty miles an hour,
with Jim Lewis running after the car and shouting, Take it easy, son. Don't open up until you get
out on the highway. The speed limit in town is
twenty-five miles an hour.

The Indian wasn't at all excited, even though I was throwing him around a good deal.

I wasn't doing it on purpose, though. It was simply that I wasn't very familiar with the manner in which the automobile worked.

You're an excellent driver, Willie, he said. It's like I said. You're an American and you were born with an instinct for mechanical contraptions like this.

We'll be in Mendota in an hour, I said. You'll see some great fishing out there.

How far is Mendota? the Indian said.

About ninety miles, I said.

Ninety miles is too far to go in an hour, the Indian said. Take two hours. We're passing a lot of interesting scenery I'd like to look at a little more closely.

All right, I said, but I sure am anxious to get out there and fish.

Well, all right then, the Indian said. Go as fast as you like this time, but some time I'll expect you to drive a little more slowly, so I can see some of the scenery. I'm missing everything. I don't even get a chance to read the signs.

I'll travel slowly *now* if you want me to, I said.

No, he insisted. Let her go. Let her go as fast as she'll go.

Well, we got out to Mendota in an hour and seventeen minutes. I would have made better time except for the long stretch of dirt road.

I drove the car right up to the river bank. The Indian asked if I knew how to get the top down, so he could sit in the open and watch me fish. I didn't know how to get the top down, but I got it down. It took me twenty minutes to do it.

I fished for about three hours, fell into the river twice, and finally landed a small one.

You don't know the first thing about fishing, the Indian said.

What am I doing wrong? I said.

Everything, he said. Have you ever fished before?

No, I said.

I didn't think so, he said.

What am I doing wrong? I said.

Well, he said, nothing in particular, only you're fishing at about the same rate of speed that you drive an automobile.

Is that wrong? I said.

It's not exactly wrong, he said, except that it'll

keep you from getting anything to speak of, and
you'll go on falling into the river.

I'm not falling, I said. They're pulling me in.
They've got an awful pull. This grass is mighty
slippery, too. There ain't nothing around here to
grab hold of.

I reeled in one more little one and then I asked
if he'd like to go home. He said he would if I
wanted to, too, so I put away the fishing equipment and the two fish and got in the car and
started driving back to town.

I drove that big Packard for this Ojibway
Indian, Locomotive 38, as long as he stayed in
town, which was all summer. He stayed at the
hotel all the time. I tried to get him to learn to
drive, but he said it was out of the question. I
drove that Packard all over the San Joaquín Valley that summer, with the Indian in the back,
chewing eight or nine sticks of gum. He told me
to drive anywhere I cared to go, so it was either
to some place where I could fish, or some place
where I could hunt. He claimed I didn't know
anything about fishing or hunting, but he was
glad to see me trying. As long as I knew him he
never laughed, except once. That was the time I
shot at a jack-rabbit with a 12-gauge shotgun that

had a terrible kick, and killed a crow. He tried to tell me all the time that that was my average. To shoot at a jack-rabbit and kill a crow. You're an American, he said. Look at the way you took to this big automobile.

One day in November that year his brother came to town from Oklahoma, and the next day when I went down to the hotel to get him, they told me he'd gone back to Oklahoma with his brother.

Where's the Packard? I said.

They took the Packard, the hotel clerk said.

Who drove? I said.

The Indian, the clerk said.

They're both Indians, I said. Which of the brothers drove the car?

The one who lived at this hotel, the clerk said.

Are you sure? I said.

Well, I only saw him get into the car out front and drive away, the clerk said. That's all.

Do you mean to tell me he knew how to shift gears? I said.

It *looked* as if he did, the clerk said. He looked like an expert driver to me.

Thanks, I said.

On the way home I figured he'd just wanted

me to *believe* he couldn't drive, so *I* could drive all the time and feel good. He was just a young man who'd come to town on a donkey, bored to death or something, who'd taken advantage of the chance to be entertained by a small town kid who was bored to death, too. That's the only way I could figure it out without accepting the general theory that he was crazy.

OLD COUNTRY ADVICE TO

THE AMERICAN TRAVELER

ONE year my uncle Melik traveled from Fresno to New York. Before he got aboard the train his uncle Garro paid him a visit and told him about the dangers of travel.

When you get on the train, the old man said, choose your seat carefully, sit down, and do not look about.

Yes, sir, my uncle said.

Several moments after the train begins to move, the old man said, two men wearing uniforms will come down the aisle and ask you for your ticket. Ignore them. They will be impostors.

How will I know? my uncle said.

You will know, the old man said. You are no longer a child.

Yes, sir, my uncle said.

Before you have traveled twenty miles an ami‑

able young man will come to you and offer you a cigarette. Tell him you don't smoke. The cigarette will be doped.

Yes, sir, said my uncle.

On your way to the diner a very beautiful young woman will bump into you intentionally and almost embrace you, the old man said. She will be extremely apologetic and attractive, and your natural impulse will be to cultivate her friendship. Dismiss your natural impulse and go on in and eat. The woman will be an adventuress.

A what? my uncle said.

A whore, the old man shouted. Go on in and eat. Order the best food, and if the diner is crowded, and the beautiful young woman sits across the table from you, do not look into her eyes. If she speaks, pretend to be deaf.

Yes, sir, my uncle said.

Pretend to be deaf, the old man said. That is the only way out of it.

Out of what? my uncle said.

Out of the whole ungodly mess, the old man said. I have traveled. I know what I'm talking about.

Yes, sir, my uncle said.

Let's say no more about it, the old man said.

Yes, sir, my uncle said.

Let's not speak of the matter again, the old man said. It's finished. I have seven children. My life has been a full and righteous one. Let's not give it another thought. I have land, vines, trees, cattle, and money. One cannot have everything—except for a day or two at a time.

Yes, sir, my uncle said.

On your way back to your seat from the diner, the old man said, you will pass through the smoker. There you will find a game of cards in progress. The players will be three middle-aged men with expensive-looking rings on their fingers. They will nod at you pleasantly and one of them will invite you to join the game. Tell them, No speak English.

Yes, sir, my uncle said.

That is all, the old man said.

Thank you very much, my uncle said.

One thing more, the old man said. When you go to bed at night, take your money out of your pocket and put it in your shoe. Put your shoe under your pillow, keep your head on the pillow all night, *and don't sleep.*

Yes, sir, my uncle said.

That is all, the old man said.

The old man went away and the next day my uncle Melik got aboard the train and traveled straight across America to New York. The two men in uniforms were not impostors, the young man with the doped cigarette did not arrive, the beautiful young woman did not sit across the table from my uncle in the diner, and there was no card game in progress in the smoker. My uncle put his money in his shoe and put his shoe under his pillow and put his head on the pillow and didn't sleep all night the first night, but the second night he abandoned the whole ritual.

The second day he *himself* offered another young man a cigarette which the other young man accepted. In the diner my uncle went out of his way to sit at a table with a young lady. He started a poker game in the smoker, and long before the train ever got to New York my uncle knew everybody aboard the train and everybody knew him. Once, while the train was traveling through Ohio, my uncle and the young man who had accepted the cigarette and two young ladies on their way to Vassar formed a quartette and sang *The Wabash Blues.*

The journey was a very pleasant one.

When my uncle Melik came back from New York, his old uncle Garro visited him again.

I see you are looking all right, he said. Did you follow my instructions?

Yes, sir, my uncle said.

The old man looked far away in space.

I am pleased that *someone* has profited by my experience, he said.

THE POOR AND BURNING

ARAB

MY uncle Khosrove, himself a man of furious energy and uncommon sadness, had for a friend one year a small man from the old country who was as still as a rock inwardly, whose sadness was expressed by brushing a speck of dust from his knee and never speaking.

This man was an Arab named Khalil. He was no bigger than a boy of eight, but, like my uncle Khosrove, had a very big mustache. He was probably in his early sixties. In spite of his mustache, however, he impressed one as being closer to a child in heart than to a man. His eyes were the eyes of a child, but seemed to be full of years of remembrance—years and years of being separated from things deeply loved, as perhaps his native land, his father, his mother, his brother, his horse, or something else. The hair on his head was soft and thick and as black as black ever was, and

parted on the left side, the way small boys who
had just reached America from the old country
were taught by their parents to part their hair.
His head was, in fact, the head of a schoolboy,
except for the mustache, and so was his body, except for the broad shoulders. He could speak no
English, only a little Turkish, a few words of
Kurdish, and only a few of Armenian, but he
hardly ever spoke anyway. When he did, he spoke
in a voice that seemed to come not so much from
himself as from the old country. He spoke, also,
as if he regretted the necessity to do so, as if it
were pathetic for one to try to express what could
never be expressed, as if anything he might say
would only add to the sorrow already existing in
himself.

How he won the regard of my uncle Khosrove,
a man who *had* to say *something* at least, is a thing
none of us ever learned. Little enough is learned
from people who are always talking, let alone
from people who hardly ever talk, except, as in
the case of my uncle Khosrove, to swear or demand that someone else stop talking. My uncle
Khosrove probably met the Arab at the Arax
Coffee House.

My uncle Khosrove picked his friends and

enemies from the way they played *tavli*, which in this country is known as backgammon. Games of any sort are tests of human behavior under stress, and, even though my uncle Khosrove himself was probably the worst loser in the world, he despised any other man who lost without grace.

What are you grieving about? he would shout at such a loser. It's a game, isn't it? Do you lose your life with it?

He himself lost *his* life when he lost a game, but it was inconceivable to him that anyone else might regard the symbols of the game as profoundly as he did. To the others the game was *only* a game, as far as he was concerned. To himself, however, the game was destiny—over a board on a table, with an insignificant man across the table rattling the dice, talking to them in Turkish, coaxing them, whispering, shouting, and in many other ways humiliating himself.

My uncle Khosrove, on the other hand, despised the dice, regarded them as his personal enemies, and never spoke to them. He threw them out of the window or across the room, and pushed the board off the table.

The dogs! he would shout.

And then, pointing furiously at his opponent,

he would shout, And you! My own countryman! You are not ashamed. You debase yourself before them. You pray to them. I am ashamed for you. I spit on the dogs.

Naturally, no one ever played a game of *tavli* with my uncle Khosrove twice.

This Coffee House was a place of great fame and importance in its day. In this day it is the same, although many have died who went there twenty years ago.

For the most part the place was frequented by Armenians, but others came, too. All who remembered the old country. All who loved it. All who had played *tavli* and the card game *scambile* in the old country. All who enjoyed the food of the old country, the wine, the *rakhi,* and the small cups of coffee in the afternoons. All who loved the songs, and the stories. And all who liked to be in a place with a familiar smell, thousands of miles from home.

Most of the time my uncle Khosrove reached this place around three in the afternoon. He would stand a moment looking over the men, and then sit down in a corner, alone. He usually sat an hour, without moving, and then would go away, terribly angry, although no one had said a word to him.

Poor little ones, he would say. Poor little orphans. Or, literally, Poor and burning orphans.

Poor and burning—it's impossible to translate this one. Nothing, however, is more sorrowful than the *poor and burning* in life and in the world.

Most likely, sitting in this Coffee House one day, my uncle Khosrove noticed the little Arab, and knew him to be a man of worth. Perhaps the man had been seated, playing *tavli*, his broad shoulders over the board, his child's head somber and full of understanding and regret, and perhaps after the game my uncle Khosrove had seen him get up and stand, no bigger than a child.

It may even be that the man came to the Coffee House and, not knowing my uncle Khosrove, played a game of *tavli* with him and *lost*, and did not complain; and, in fact, understood *who* my uncle Khosrove was—without being told. It may even be that the Arab did not pray to the dice.

Whatever the source of their friendship, whatever the understanding between the two, and whatever the communion they shared, they were at any rate together occasionally in our parlor, and welcome.

✦

The first time my uncle Khosrove brought the Arab to our house, he neglected to introduce him. My mother assumed that the Arab was a country-man of ours, perhaps a distant cousin, although he was a little darker than most of the members of our tribe, and smaller. Which, of course, was no matter; nothing more than the charm of a people; the variety; the quality which made them human and worthy of further extension in time.

The Arab sat down that first day only after my mother had asked him a half-dozen times to be at home.

Was he deaf? she thought.

No, it was obvious that he could hear; he listened so intently.

Perhaps he didn't understand our dialect. My mother asked what city he was from. He did not reply, except to brush dust from the sleeve of his coat. Then in Turkish my mother said, Are you an Armenian? This the Arab understood; he replied in Turkish that he was an Arab.

A poor and burning little orphan, my uncle Khosrove whispered.

The Poor and Burning Arab

For a moment my mother imagined that the Arab might wish to speak, but it was soon obvious that, like my uncle Khosrove, nothing grieved him more than to do so. He could, if necessary, speak, but there was simply nothing, in all truth, to say.

My mother took the two men tobacco, and coffee, and motioned to me to leave.

They want to talk, she said.

Talk? I said.

They want to be alone, she said.

I sat at the table in the dining room and began turning the pages of a year-old copy of the *Saturday Evening Post* that I knew by heart—especially the pictures: Jello, very architectural; automobiles, with high-toned people standing around; flashlights flashing into dark places; tables set with bowls of soup steaming; young men in fancy ready-made suits and coats; and all sorts of other pictures.

I must have turned the pages a little too quickly, however.

My uncle Khosrove shouted, Quiet, boy, quiet.

I looked into the parlor just in time to see the Arab brushing dust from his knee.

The two men sat in the parlor an hour, and

then the Arab breathed very deeply through his nose and without a word left the house.

I went into the parlor and sat where he had sat.

What is his name? I said.

Quiet, my uncle Khosrove said.

Well, what is his name? I said.

My uncle Khosrove was so irritated he didn't know what to do. He called out to my mother, as if he were being murdered.

Mariam! he shouted. Mariam!

My mother hurried into the parlor.

What is it? she said.

Send him away—please, my uncle Khosrove said.

What is the matter?

He wants to know the Arab's name.

Well, all right, my mother said. He's a child. He's curious. Tell him.

I see, my uncle Khosrove groaned. You, too. My own sister. My own poor and burning little sister.

Well, what is the Arab's name? my mother said.

I won't tell, my uncle Khosrove said. That's all. I won't tell.

He got up and left the house.

He doesn't know the man's name, my mother

explained. And you've got no business irritating him.

Three days later when my uncle Khosrove and the Arab came to our house I was in the parlor.

My uncle Khosrove came straight to me and said, His name is Khalil. Now go away.

I left the house and waited in the yard for one of my cousins to arrive. After ten minutes, nobody arrived, so I went to my cousin Mourad's house and spent an hour arguing with him about which of us would be the stronger in five years. We wrestled three times and I lost three times, but once I *almost* won.

When I got home the two men were gone. I ran straight to the parlor from the back of the house, but they weren't there. The only thing in the room was their smell and the smell of tobacco smoke.

What did they talk about? I asked my mother.

I didn't listen, my mother said.

Did they talk at all? I said.

I don't know, my mother said.

They didn't, I said.

Some people talk when they have something to say, my mother said, and some people don't.

How can you talk if you don't say anything? I said.

You talk without words. We are always talking without words.

Well, what good are words, then?

Not very good, most of the time. Most of the time they're only good to keep back what you really want to say, or something you don't want known.

Well, do *they* talk? I said.

I think they do, my mother said. They just sit and sip coffee and smoke cigarettes. They never open their mouths, but they're talking all the time. They understand one another and don't need to open their mouths. They have nothing to keep back.

Do they really know what they're talking about? I said.

Of course, my mother said.

Well, what is it? I said.

I can't tell you, my mother said, because it isn't in words; but they know.

✦

For a year my uncle Khosrove and the Arab came to our house every now and then and sat in

204

the parlor. Sometimes they sat an hour, sometimes two.

Once my uncle Khosrove suddenly shouted at the Arab, *Pay no attention to it, I tell you,* although the Arab had said nothing.

But most of the time nothing at all was said until it was time for them to go. Then my uncle Khosrove would say quietly, The poor and burning orphans, and the Arab would brush dust from his knee.

One day when my uncle Khosrove came to our house alone, I realized that the Arab had not visited our house in several months.

Where is the Arab? I said.

What Arab? my uncle Khosrove said.

That poor and burning little Arab that used to come here with you, I said. Where is he?

Mariam! my uncle Khosrove shouted. He was standing, terrified.

Oh-oh, I thought. What's wrong now? What have I done now?

Mariam! he shouted. Mariam!

My mother came into the parlor.

What is it? she said.

If you please, my uncle Khosrove said. He is your son. You are my little sister. Please send him away. I love him with all my heart. He is an American. He was born here. He will be a great man some day. I have no doubt about it. Please send him away.

Why, what is it? my mother said.

What is it? *What is it?* He talks. He asks questions. I love him.

Aram, my mother said.

I was standing too, and if my uncle Khosrove was angry at me, I was angrier at him.

Where is the Arab? I said.

My uncle Khosrove pointed me out to my mother—with despair. There you are, his gesture said. Your son. My nephew. My own flesh and blood. You see? We are all poor and burning orphans. All except *him*.

Aram, my mother said.

Well, if you don't talk, I said, I can't understand. *Where is the Arab?*

My uncle Khosrove left the house without a word.

The Arab is dead, my mother said.

When did he tell you? I said.

He didn't tell me, my mother said.

Well, how did you find out? I said.

The Poor and Burning Arab

I don't know how, my mother said, but he is dead.

My uncle Khosrove didn't visit our house again for many days. For a while I thought he would *never* come back. When he came at last he stood in the parlor with his hat on his head and said, The Arab is dead. He died an orphan in an alien world, six thousand miles from home. He wanted to go home and die. He wanted to see his sons again. He wanted to talk to them again. He wanted to smell them. He wanted to hear them breathing. He had no money. He used to think about them all the time. Now he is dead. Now go away. I love you.

I wanted to ask some more questions, especially about the Arab's sons, how many there were, how long he had been away from them, and so on, but I decided I would rather visit my cousin Mourad and see if I couldn't hold him down *now,* so I went away without saying a word—which most likely pleased my uncle Khosrove very much, and made him feel maybe there was some hope for me, after all.

A WORD TO SCOFFERS

FROM Reno to Salt Lake City all you get to see from a bus or any other kind of conveyance is desert, and in August all you feel is dry heat. Desert is sand spread out evenly in every direction, different kinds of cactus, and the sun. Sometimes the sand looks white, sometimes brown, and around sundown the color of the sand changes from white or brown to yellow, and then black. Then it is night, and that is when the desert is best of all. When the desert and night join one another you get what amounts to silence.

This is a thing you remember and remember.

The remembrance is full of the hush and mystery of the world.

I know all this because I rode in a bus from Reno to Salt Lake City once, on my way to New York.

My uncle Gyko told me to get out of town and

go to New York. He said, Don't stay in these little town. Go to Nor York. I tell you, Aram, eat ease insanity.

That's how it happened that I rode in the bus from Reno to Salt Lake City.

That was country I had never seen, or imagined. Wide dry waste-land, full of nothing. I kept my eyes open night and day watching that country. I didn't want to pass through country like that without finding out all I could about it.

The bus left Reno a little after midnight. Reno is one of those American towns that lives on nothing but the disease of people. The only thing there is gambling and whoring.

Consequently, the city lights are bright.

I remember going into a gambling joint and seeing clearly all the way from the rail to the poker game in the corner of the room the three black hairs growing out of the dealer's nose. It was that light.

Then the bus rolled out of Reno into the desert. That was a mighty remarkable difference to dwell upon: first the bright lights of the gambling joints of Reno, and then the desert at night. I dwelt on those bright lights and the desert from midnight till morning, and even then I didn't find out enough for one small sentence of three words.

All I did in the morning was yawn. When the bus stopped, I got out and had a good look. Well, all it was was dirt and sky, and the sun coming up. I couldn't think of three little words with which to clarify the situation. It was nothing. That's all. Nothing at all. No streets, no buildings, no corners, no doorways, no doors, no windows, no signs, nothing.

My uncle Gyko told me not to stay in a small town like the small town I was born in, and now I couldn't wait to get out of the desert into a big town and be able to understand something again. I began to figure it wouldn't do my uncle Gyko any harm to get out of our small town and pass through the desert himself. I figured he might not be so sure about everything if he got himself all surrounded by the desert, day and night, and felt that sullen silence. My uncle Gyko hadn't read as many smart books as I had read because he read slower and with greater difficulty, but he had read everything he had read very carefully and memorized whole pages of the works of writers who had lived in Europe as long as two hundred years ago. In his own broken-English way he used to cut loose with a lot of derivative invective. He used to call people sheep, and claim that he himself wasn't a sheep. I myself was just as wise as my uncle Gyko, only I didn't speak with an accent. My uncle Gyko said, Get out of these town and go to Nor York.

I figured my uncle Gyko ought to visit the desert himself and see how *he* felt. I figured I couldn't figure out anything in a place so empty as all that. I didn't feel like feeling smart at all. I felt lonely, too. That's why I tried to start a conversation with the only girl on the bus, inexperienced as I was in the art of polite conversation.

What's the name of this place? I said to the girl. She was at least thirty-five and very ugly.

What place? the girl said.

All this land around here, I said.

I don't know, the girl said.

That was as far as the conversation went until late the next afternoon when the girl asked me what time it was and I said I didn't know.

I didn't even know what day it was. I was beginning to find out that all I knew was that I didn't know anything, and wanted to get to Salt Lake City as soon as possible so I could see streets and places again and people walking around, and maybe get back my tremendous book-learning that was so useless in the desert.

Just let me get to a city again, I said, and I'll be as smart as the next fellow. Maybe smarter. Just get me out of this desolation and I'll start throwing wise cracks all over the place.

Well, I was wrong. When I got to Salt Lake City I felt more confused than ever. I couldn't find a room for fifty cents, or a restaurant where I could get a big dinner for fifteen cents. I felt tired and hungry and sleepy and sore at the people in the streets, and the buildings there, and I wished to Christ I hadn't left home.

I paid a dollar for a little room in an old hotel. The room turned out to be haunted. It was the toughest room I ever tried to stay in, but I used to be very stubborn in those days and I stayed in the room until I could see every kind of evil form that never in the history of the world reached material substance, and could hear every kind of awful sound that science insisted didn't exist. I was scared stiff. In two hours I didn't move from the rocking-chair in the middle of the room because I was sure something would grab hold of me and strangle me before I could get to the door or window. The room was full of evil things. I don't know how I got out of it alive, but I got out all right.

I walked through the streets of Salt Lake City and found a restaurant where you could get a hamburger dinner for a quarter.

After dinner, I went back to that little room in that little hotel and got in bed without taking off any of my clothes, not even my shoes or my hat. I wanted to be ready to sprint in case of riot, fire, earthquake, flood, pestilence, or any other kind of emergency. Before turning out the light I practiced getting out of the bed and getting to the door. I was making it in record-breaking time, one jump to the door, and maybe three or four seconds to the street. I left the room only three times during the course of the night, but awoke in the morning refreshed and cheerful.

I got up at five in the morning because I didn't want to miss the bus that was leaving town at half past nine.

At a quarter past nine I was standing in front of the bus depot, smoking a five cent cigar, trying to get back my young irreligious poise so that I could be happy again when a very tall and melancholy-looking man of fifty in overalls handed me a little pamphlet and said, Son, are you saved?

A Word to Scoffers

I had never before seen such a melancholy-looking man. Six feet two or three, no more than a hundred and twenty pounds, unshaved, and full of religion. I figured he was going to ask me for a dime because he looked more like a hungry tramp than a holy man, but all he did was hand me that religious pamphlet and ask if I was saved. The title of the little story on the pamphlet was *A Word to Scoffers,* and the missionary had found his man all right. I didn't know. I couldn't tell at the time. I was all mixed up.

I took a sophisticated puff on the nickel cigar and said, No, I don't think I'm saved, but I'm sympathetic.

Brother, said the religious man, I can save you through the gospel of Brigham Young.

I'm leaving town in fifteen minutes, I said.

That's all right, said the religious man. I once saved a man in four minutes.

That's fast work, I said. What do I have to do to get saved?

Son, said the religious man, you don't have to do anything. You have no idea how close to being saved every man alive is. Any man you can think of. I used to be something of a rounder myself, snappy clothes, strong drink, panatela cigars, cards, dice, horses, sporting girls. Everything. Changed over-night.

Why? I said.

Lost my luck and couldn't sleep, said the religious man. Fell to thinking and found out I never was intended to be an enemy of the truth.

What truth? I said.

God's *holy* truth, said the missionary. No man is ever much of an enemy of the truth. All them crazy things people do is because they don't know what they're after.

Well, what *are* they after? I said.

Truth, he said. Every man who cheats at cards, carries on with women, holds up a bank, gets drunk, or travels, is looking for truth. I guess you're going somewhere, son. Where you going?

I'm on my way to New York, I said.

Well, he said, you won't find any truth there. I been there six times in the last thirty years. You can go hopping around all over the world and never find out anything because that ain't the way you find out anything. All you got to do is change your attitude.

That ought to be easy, I said.

Easiest thing in the world, he said.

I'm game, I said. I've got nothing to lose. How do I change my attitude?

Well, said the religious man, you stop trying to figure things out and you *believe*.

Believe, I said. Believe *what?*

Why, everything, he said. Everything you can think of, left, right, north, east, south, west, upstairs, downstairs and all around, inside, out, visible, invisible, good and bad and neither and both. That's the little secret. Took me fifty years to find out.

Is that all I have to do? I said.

That's all, son, said the missionary.

O.K., I said. *I believe.*

Son, said the religious man, you're saved. You can go to New York now or anywhere else, and everything will be smooth and easy.

I hope you're right, I said.

You'll find out, said the religious man.

The big bus came to the curb and I got in. The lanky man of God came to the window, smiling proudly.

You're the fifty-seventh man I've saved, he said.

Well, so long, I said. Many thanks for the little secret.

Glad to do it, he said. Only don't forget. Just believe.

I won't forget, I said. I'll believe.

Anything, he said.

The motor of the bus started.

Any old thing at all, I said.

The bus belched smoke and slowly rolled away.

I thought I was kidding the old padre of Salt Lake City, getting back my vast book-learning and anti-religious poise, but I was sadly mistaken, because unwittingly I *had* been saved. In less than ten minutes after the bus left Salt Lake City I was believing everything, left and right, as the missionary had said, and it's been that way with me ever since.